The McKenna Brothers

Three billionaire brothers.
Three guarded hearts. Three fabulous stories.

Meet the gorgeous McKenna Brothers in this brand-new trilogy from the wonderfully witty *New York Times* bestselling author Shirley Jump.

Rich, handsome and successful, they're the most eligible bachelors in Boston!

Find out what happens when the oldest brother, Finn, finds himself propositioned by the intriguing, feisty Ellie Winston in

One Day to Find a Husband
July 2012

Discover whether straight-talking Stace Kettering can tame notorious playboy Riley in

How the Playboy Got Serious
August 2012

Returning hero Brody is back home and has a secret…but can he confide in Kate Spencer? Find out in

Return of the Last McKenna
September 2012

Dear Reader,

I'm almost sad to write this Dear Reader letter because it means the McKenna brothers trilogy has come to an end. I loved each and every brother, and had a lot of fun writing their stories. Not only did these books let me return home to the place where I grew up, but they also presented lots of challenges and interesting story lines.

Heidi, the dog who first appears in Finn's book, is based on my own real-life golden retriever, who died a few years ago. I enjoyed being able to bring her to life again on the page and having her become a big part of the McKenna family. But most of all, I really enjoyed writing about the military and its heroes. My father is retired from the military, and my husband is former military, so the sacrifice our troops make every day is very dear to me. I hope you enjoy Brody's story, and can relate to Elena's grandma's addiction to cupcakes (that one is all, uh, me. I love cupcakes!).

I love to hear from readers, so please visit my website (www.shirleyjump.com) or visit my blog (www.shirleyjump.blogspot.com), where I share family recipes and writing news. Stop on by and share a recipe, a favorite book, or just say hello!

Happy reading!

Shirley

SHIRLEY JUMP

Return of the Last McKenna

HARLEQUIN®
entertain, enrich, inspire™

Recycling programs
for this product may
not exist in your area.

ISBN-13: 978-0-373-17833-9

RETURN OF THE LAST McKENNA

First North American Publication 2012

Copyright © 2012 by Shirley Kawa-Jump, LLC

This edition published by arrangement with Harlequin Books S.A.

For questions and comments about the quality of this book
please contact us at CustomerService@Harlequin.com.

www.Harlequin.com

Printed in U.S.A.

New York Times bestselling author **Shirley Jump** didn't have the willpower to diet or the talent to master under-eye concealer, so she bowed out of a career in television and opted instead for a career where she could be paid to eat at her desk—writing. At first, seeking revenge on her children for their grocery-store tantrums, she sold embarrassing essays about them to anthologies. However, it wasn't enough to feed her growing addiction to writing funny. So she turned to the world of romance novels, where messes are (usually) cleaned up before The End. In the worlds Shirley gets to create and control, the children listen to their parents, the husbands always remember holidays and the housework is magically done by elves. Though she's thrilled to see her books in stores around the world, Shirley mostly writes because it gives her an excuse to avoid cleaning the toilets and helps feed her shoe habit.

To learn more, visit her website at www.shirleyjump.com.

Books by Shirley Jump

HOW THE PLAYBOY GOT SERIOUS*
ONE DAY TO FIND A HUSBAND*
THE PRINCESS TEST
HOW TO LASSO A COWBOY
IF THE RED SLIPPER FITS
VEGAS PREGNANCY SURPRISE
BEST MAN SAYS I DO

*The McKenna Brothers trilogy

Other titles by this author available in ebook format.

To the most heroic military man I know—
my husband, who served his country, and has
made me proud to be his wife in a thousand
different ways. Not to mention, he's the kind
of guy who brings home cupcakes just because
I had a hard day. He knows me well!

CHAPTER ONE

BRODY McKenna checked his third sore throat of the morning, prescribed the same prescription as he had twice before—rest, fluids, acetaminophen—and tried to count his blessings. He had a dependable job as a family physician, a growing practice, and a close knit family living nearby. He'd returned from his time overseas none the worse for wear, and should have been excited to get back to his job.

He wasn't.

The six-year-old patient headed out the door, with a sugar-free lollipop and a less harried mother. As they left, Helen Maguire, the nurse who had been with him since day one, and with Doc Watkins for fifteen years before that, poked her head in the door. "That's the last patient of the morning," she said. A matronly figure in pink scrubs decorated with zoo animals, Mrs. Maguire had short gray hair and a smile for every patient, young or old. "We have an hour until it's time to start immunizations. And then later in the afternoon, we'll be doing sports physicals."

Brody's mind drifted away from his next appointment and the flurry of activity in his busy Newton office. His gaze swept the room, the jars of supplies, so easy to order and stock here in America, always on hand and ready for any emergency. Every bandage, every tongue depressor, every stethoscope, reminded him. Launched him back to a hot country and a dusty dirt floor hut short on supplies and even shorter on miracles.

"Doc? Did you hear me?" Mrs. Maguire asked.

"Oh, oh. Yes. Sorry." Brody washed his hands, then dried them and handed the chart to Helen. Focus on work, he told himself, not on a moment in the past that couldn't be changed. Or on a country on the other side of the world, to those people he couldn't save.

Especially not on that.

"Lots of colds going around," he said.

"It's that time of year."

"I think it's always that time of year."

Helen shrugged. "I think that's what I like about family practice. You can set your watch by the colds and flus and shots. It has a certain rhythm to it, don't you think?"

"I do." For a long time, Brody had thought he had the perfect life. A family practice for a family man.

Or at least, that had been the plan. Then the family had dissolved before it had a chance to form. By that time, Brody had already stepped into Doc Watkins's shoes. Walking away from a thriving practice would be insane, so he'd stayed. For a long time, he'd been happy. He liked the patients. Liked working with kids, liked seeing the families grow and change.

It was good work, and he took satisfaction in that, and had augmented it with volunteer time with different places over the years—a clinic in Alabama, a homeless shelter in Maine. When the opportunity to volunteer assisting the remaining military overseas arose, Brody had jumped at it.

For a month, he'd changed lives in Afghanistan, working side by side with other docs in a roving medical unit that visited villagers too poor to get to a doctor or hospital, with the American military along for protection.

Brody had thought he'd make a difference there, too. He had—just not in the way he wanted. And now he couldn't find peace, no matter where he turned.

"You okay, doc?" Mrs. Maguire asked.

"Fine." His gaze landed on the jars of supplies again. "Just distracted. I think I'll head out for lunch instead of eating at my desk."

And being around all these reminders.

"No problem. It'll do you good to take some time to enjoy the day." Mrs. Maguire smiled. "I find a little fresh air can make everything seem brighter."

Brody doubted the air would work any miracles for him, but maybe some space and distance would. Unfortunately, he had little of either. "I'll be back by one."

He stepped outside his office and into a warm, almost summer day. The temperatures still lingered in the high seventies, even though the calendar date read deep into September. Brody headed down the street, waving to the neighbors who flanked his Newton practice—Mr. Simon with his shoe repair shop, Mrs. Tipp with her art gallery and Milo, who had opened three different types of shops in the same location, like an entrepreneur with ADD.

Brody took the same path as he took most days when he walked during his lunch hour. He rarely ate, just walked from his office to the same destination and back. He'd done it so many times in the last few weeks, he half expected to see a worn river of footsteps down the center of the sidewalk.

Brody reached in his pocket as he rounded the corner. The paper was crinkled and worn, the edges beginning to fray, but the inked message had stayed clear.

Hey, Superman, take care of yourself and come home safe. People over here love and miss you. Especially me. Things just aren't the same without your goofy face around. Love you, Kate.

Brody had held onto that card for a month now. He ran his hands over the letters now, and debated the same thing he'd had in his head for weeks. To fulfill Andrew's last wishes, or let it go?

He paused. His feet had taken him to the same destination as always. He stood under the bright red and white awning of Nora's Sweet Shop and debated again, the card firm in his grip.

Promise me, Doc. Promise me you'll go see her. Make sure she's okay. Make sure she's happy. But please, don't tell her what happened. She'll blame herself and Kate has suffered enough already.

The promise had been easy to make a month ago. Harder to keep.

Brody fingered the card again. *Promise me.*

How many times had he made this journey and turned back instead of taking, literally, the next step?

If he returned to the thermometers and stethoscopes and bandages, though, would he ever find peace?

He knew that answer. No. He needed to do this. Step forward instead of back.

Brody took a deep breath, then opened the door and stepped inside the shop. The sweet scents of chocolate and vanilla drifted over him, while soft jazz music filled his ears. A glass case of cupcakes and chocolates sat at one end of the store while a bright rainbow of gift baskets lined the sides. A cake made out of cupcakes and decorated in bridal colors sat on a glass stand in a bay window. Along the top of the walls ran a border of dark pink writing trimmed with chocolate brown and a hand lettered script reading Nora's Sweet Shop. On the wall behind the counter, hung a framed spatula with the name of the shop carved in the handle.

"Just a minute!" a woman called from the back.

"No problem," Brody said, stuffing the card back into his pocket. "I'm just…"

Just what? Not browsing. Not looking for candy or cupcakes. And he sure as hell couldn't say the truth—

He'd come to this little shop in downtown Newton for forgiveness.

So instead he grabbed the first assembled basket of treats he saw and marched over to the counter. He was just pulling out his wallet when a slim brunette woman emerged from the back room.

"Hi, I'm Kate." She dried her hands on the front of her apron before proffering one for him to shake. "How can I help you?"

Kate Spencer. The owner of the shop, and the woman he'd thought of a hundred times in the past weeks. A woman he'd never met but heard enough about to write at least a couple chapters of her biography.

He took her hand, a steady, firm grip—and tried not to stare. All these weeks he'd held onto that card, he'd expected someone, well, someone like a young version of Mrs. Maguire. A motherly type with her hair in a bun, and an apron around her waist, and a hug ready for anyone she met. That was how Andrew had made his older sister sound. Loving, warm, dependable. Like a down comforter.

Not the thin, fit, dynamo who had hurried out of the back room, with a friendly smile on her face and her coffee colored hair in a sassy ponytail skewed a bit too far to the right. She had deep green eyes, full crimson lips and delicate, pretty features. Yet he saw shadows dusting the undersides of her eyes and a tension in her shoulders.

Brody opened his mouth to introduce himself, to fulfill his purpose for being here, but the words wouldn't get past his throat. "I…I…uh," he glanced down at the counter, at the cellophane package in his hands, "I wanted to get this."

"No problem. Is it for a special person?"

Brody's mind raced for an answer. "My, uh, grandmother. She loves chocolate."

"Your grandma?" Kate laughed, then spun the basket to face him. "You want me to, ah, change out this bow? To something a little more feminine? Unless your grandma is a big fan?"

He glanced down and noticed he'd chosen a basket with a Red Sox ribbon. The dark blue basket with red trim, filled with white foil wrapped chocolates shaped like baseballs and bats, couldn't be further from the type of thing his staid grandmother liked. He chuckled. "No, that'd be me. I've even got season tickets. When she does watch baseball, my grandma is strictly a Yankees fan, though you can't say that too loud in Boston."

Kate laughed, a light lyrical, happy sound. Again, Brody realized how far off his imaginings of her had been. "Well, Mr. Red Sox, let me make this more grandma friendly. Okay? And meanwhile, if you want to put a card with this, there are some on the counter over there."

"Thanks." He wandered over to the counter she'd indicated, and tugged out a card, then scribbled his name across it. That kept him from watching her and gave his brain a few minutes to adjust to the reality of Kate Spencer.

She was, in a word, beautiful. The kind of woman, on any other day, he might have asked out on a date. Friendly, sweet natured, with a ready smile and a teasing lilt to her words. Her smile had roused something in him the minute he saw her, and that surprised him. He hadn't expected to be attracted to her, not one bit.

He tried to find a way around to say what he had come to say. *Promise me.*

He'd practiced the words he needed to say in his head a hundred times, but now that the moment had arrived, they wouldn't come. It wasn't the kind of subject one could just dump in the middle of a business transaction, nor had he quite figured out how to fulfill Andrew's wishes without giving away why. He needed to lead up to it, somehow. Yeah, easier to climb Mt. Everest.

"So…how's business?" he asked.

"Pretty good. We've been growing every year since

we opened in 1953. Mondays are our only slow day of the week. Almost like a mini vacation, except at the beginning of the week."

"You make all the cupcakes and candy things your-self?"

She shook her head and laughed. "I couldn't. It's a lot of work. Nora's Sweet Shop has been a family busi-ness for many years, but…" she trailed off, seemed to look elsewhere for a second, then came back, "anyway, now I have a helper who's invaluable in the kitchen. Why, you applying?"

"Me? I'm all thumbs in the kitchen."

"That can be dangerous if there are knives involved." She grinned. "But seriously, baking is something you can learn. I never had formal training. Learned it all at my grandmother's knee. And if a hopeless case like me can grow up to be a baker, anyone can."

"Sounds like you love working here."

"I do. It's…therapeutic." The humor dimmed in her features, and her gaze again went to somewhere he couldn't see. He didn't have to be psychic to know why sadness had washed over her face. Because of choices Brody had made on the other side of the world.

Damn.

Brody cleared his throat. "Work can be good for the soul."

Or at least, that's what he told himself every time he walked into his practice. Ever since he'd returned from Afghanistan, though, he hadn't found that same satis-faction in his job as before. Maybe he just needed more time. That's what Mrs. Maguire said. Give it time, and it'll all get better.

"And what work do you do, that feeds your soul?"

She colored. "Sorry. That's a little personal. You don't have to answer. I was just curious."

"I'm a doctor," he said.

She leaned against the counter, one elbow on the glass, her body turned toward his. "That's a rewarding job. So much more so than baking. And not to mention, a lot more complicated than measuring out cupcake batter."

"Oh, I don't know about that," he said. "Your job looks pretty rewarding to me. I mean, you make people happy."

"It takes a lot of sugar to do that." She laughed. "But thank you. I try my best. Three generations of Spencers have been trying to do that here."

Brody's gaze drifted over the articles on the wall. Several contained accolades and positive reviews for the sweet shop, a third generation business that had enjoyed decades of raves, as evidenced by some of the framed, yellowed clippings. Brody paused when he got to the last article on the right. The page was creased on one side, as if someone had kept the paper in a book for a while before posting it on the wall. A picture of a handsome young man in uniform smiled out from the corner of the article.

SHOP OWNER'S BROTHER DIES IN AFGHANISTAN

Brody didn't have to read another word to write the ending. In an instant, he was back there, in that hot, dusty hut, praying and cursing, and praying and cursing some more, while he tried to pump life back into Andrew Spencer.

And failed.

Brody could still feel the young man's chest beneath his palms. A hard balloon, going up, going down, forced into moving by Brody's hands, but no breath escaping his lips. Andrew's eyes open, sightless, empty. His life ebbing away one second at a time, while Brody watched, helpless and frustrated. Powerless.

Damn. Damn.

No amount of time would heal that wound for Kate and her family. No amount of time would make that better. What had he been thinking? How could buying a basket ever ease the pain he'd caused Kate Spencer? What had Andrew been thinking, sending Brody here?

Brody's hand went to the card in his pocket again, but this time, the cardboard corners formed sharp barbs.

"Sir? Your basket is ready."

Brody whirled around. "My basket?"

Kate laughed and held it up. The arrangement sported a new pink and white bow and the sports-themed chocolates had been changed for ones shaped like flowers. "For grandma?"

"Oh, yeah, sure, thanks." He gestured toward the article on the wall. He knew he should let it go, but he'd made a promise, and somehow, he had to find a way to keep it. Maybe then he'd be able to sleep, to find peace, and to give some to Kate Spencer, too. "You had a brother in the war?"

A shadow dropped over her features. She fiddled with the pen on the counter. "Yeah. My little brother, Andrew. He died over there last month. We all thought he was safe because the big conflict was over, but there were still dangers around every corner."

"I'm sorry." So much sorrier than he could say. He wanted to step forward, but instead Brody lingered by the counter. All the words he'd practiced in his head seemed empty, inadequate. "That must have been tough."

"It has been. In a lot of ways. But I work, and I talk to him sometimes, and I get through it." She blushed. "That sounds crazy, I know."

"No, it doesn't. Not at all."

She smoothed a hand over the counter. "He used to work here. And I miss seeing him every day. He was the organized one in the family, and he'd be appalled at the condition of my office." She laughed, then nodded toward the basket. "Anyway, do you want to put your card with that?"

"Oh, yeah, sure." He handed Kate the message he'd scribbled to his grandmother and watched as she tucked the small paper inside the cellophane wrapper. Again, he tried to find the words he needed to say, and again, he failed. "I've, uh, never been to this place before. Lived in this neighborhood for a while and I've seen it often, but never stopped by."

"Well, thank you for coming and shopping at Nora's Sweet Shop." She gave the basket a friendly pat. "I hope your grandmother enjoys her treats."

"I'm sure she will." For the hundredth time he told himself to leave. And for the hundredth time, he didn't. "So if you're Kate, who's Nora?" He asked the question, even though he knew the answer. Andrew had talked about Nora's Sweet Shop often, and told Brody the entire story about its origins.

"Nora is my grandmother." A soft smile stole over Kate's face. "She opened this place right after my grandfather came home from the Korean War. He worked side by side with her here for sixty years before they both retired and gave the shop to my brother and me. She's the Nora in Nora's Sweet Shop and if you ask my grandfather, she's the sweet in his life."

"She's still alive?" Ever since Brody had met the jovial, brave soldier, he'd wondered what kind of people had raised a man like that. What kind of family surrounded him, supported him as he went off to defend the country.

"My grandparents are retired now," Kate said, "but they come by the shop all the time and still do some deliveries. My brother and I grew up around here, and we spent more time behind this counter than anywhere else. I think partly to help my grandparents, and partly to keep us out of trouble while my parents were working. We were mischievous when we were young," she said with a laugh, "and my brother Andrew served as my partner in crime. Back then…and also for years afterwards when we took over the shop from my grandma. He had the craziest ideas." She shook her head again. "Anyway, that's how a Kate ended up running Nora's."

Brody had heard the same story from Andrew. Both Spencer children had loved the little shop, and the indulgent grandparents who ran it. Andrew hadn't talked much about his parents, except to say they were divorced, but he had raved about his grandparents and his older sister.

It had been one of several things Brody had in common with the young soldier, and created a bond between the two of them almost from the first day they met. He'd understood that devotion to grandparents, and to siblings.

"My grandmother runs a family business, too. A marketing agency started by my grandfather years ago.

My brothers and I all went in different directions, so I think she's pinned her hopes on my cousin Alec for taking it over when she retires."

She cocked her head to one side and studied him, her gaze roaming over his suit, tie, the shiny dress shoes. A teasing smile played on her lips, danced in her eyes. Already he'd started to like Kate Spencer. Her sassy attitude, her friendly smile.

"And you, Mr. Red Sox ribbon, you are far from the business type, being a doctor?"

He chuckled. "Definitely."

"Well, should I ever feel faint," she pressed a hand to her chest and the smile widened, and something in Brody flipped inside out, "I know who to call."

For a second, he forgot his reason for being there. His gaze lingered on the hand on her chest, then drifted to the curve of her lips. "I'm right around the corner. Almost shouting distance."

"That's good to know." The smile again. "Really good."

The tension between them coiled tighter. The room warmed, and the traffic outside became a low, muted hum. Brody wished he was an ordinary customer, here on an ordinary reason. That he wasn't going to have to make that smile dim by telling her the truth.

Kate broke eye contact first. She jerked her attention to the register, her fingers hovering over the keys. "Goodness. I got so distracted by talking, I forgot to charge you."

"And I forgot to pay." Brody handed over a credit card. As he did, he noticed her hands. Long, delicate fingers tipped with no-nonsense nails. Pretty hands.

The kind that seemed like they'd have an easy, gentle touch.

She took the credit card, slid it through the register, pushed a few buttons, then waited for a receipt to print. She glanced down at his name as she handed him back the card. "Mr. McKenna, is it?"

He braced himself. Did she recognize the last name? But her smile remained friendly.

Yes, I'm Brody McKenna. The doctor who let your brother die.

Not the answer he wanted to give. Call him selfish, call him a coward, but for right now, he wanted only to see her smile again. He told himself it was because that was what Andrew had wanted, but really, Brody liked Kate's smile. A lot.

"Yes. But I prefer Brody." He scrawled his name across the receipt and slid it back to her.

"Well, thank you, Brody." His name slid off her tongue with an easy, sweet lilt. "I hope you return if you're in the neighborhood again."

"Thank you, Kate." He picked up his basket and headed for the door. As he pushed on the exit, he paused, turned back. He had come here for a reason, and had yet to fulfill even a tenth of that purpose. "Maybe someday I can return the favor."

"I didn't do anything special, just my job. If you want to return the favor, then tell all your friends to shop here and to call on us to help them celebrate special moments." And then, like a gift, she smiled at him again. "That'll be more than enough."

"No, it won't," he said, his voice low and quiet, then headed out the door.

CHAPTER TWO

WHAT had he been thinking?

He'd gone into that little shop planning...what?

To tell Kate the truth? That her little brother had charged him with making sure his sister was okay. That Brody was supposed to make sure she wasn't letting her grief overwhelm her, and that she was staying on track with her life, despite losing Andrew. Instead Brody had bought a basket of chocolates, and chickened out at the last minute. Damn.

"Tell me you're quiet because you're distracted by that pretty hostess over there," Riley said to Brody. The dim interior provided the perfect backdrop for the microbrewery/restaurant that had become their newest favorite stop for lunch. Brody had called Riley yesterday after his visit to Nora's Sweet Shop, and made plans for lunch today. That, he figured, would keep him from making another visit. And leaving without saying or doing what he'd gone there to do.

"Why are you mentioning the hostess?" Brody asked. "Aren't you getting married soon?"

"I am indeed. But that doesn't mean I can't keep my eye out for a pretty girl..." Riley leaned across the table and grinned, "for *you*. You're the last of the

McKenna boys who isn't married. Better pony up to the bar, brother, and join the club."

"No way. I've tried that—"

"You got engaged. Not married. Doesn't count. You came to the edge of the cliff and didn't jump."

"For good reason." Melissa had been more interested in the glamour of being a doctor's wife than in being *Brody's* wife. Once she'd realized he had opted for a small family practice instead of a lucrative practice like plastic surgery or cardiac care, she'd called off the engagement. She didn't want a man who spent his life "sacrificing," she'd said. No matter what Brody said or did, he couldn't fix their relationship and couldn't get it back on track. Brody's family dream had evaporated like a puddle on a summer day.

Brody picked up the menu and scanned the offerings. "How's work going?"

That drew more laughter from Riley. "Don't think I'm falling for that. You're changing the subject."

"You got me." Brody put up his hands. "I don't want to talk about the hostess or my love life or why I didn't get married. I want to visit with my little brother before he attaches the ball and chain to his ankle."

"No need for that. I'm head over heels in love with my wife to be." A goofy grin spread across Riley's face. "We're working out the final details for the wedding. Got the place—"

"The diner." A busy, quaint place in the heart of Boston where the former playboy Riley had worked for a few weeks when their grandmother had cut him off from the family pocketbook and told him to get a job and grow up. Now, a couple of months later, Riley had turned into a different man. Stace had brought out the best in Brody's little brother.

"Gran had a fit about us having the wedding at the Morning Glory, because she wanted us to get married at the Park Plaza, but Stace and I love that old diner, so it seemed only fitting we seal the deal there. Stace has her dress, though I am forbidden from seeing it until the wedding day. And you guys all have your suits—"

"Thank you again for not making me put on a tux."

Riley grinned. "You know me, Brody. I'd rather wear a horsehair shirt than a tux. Finn's the only formal one out of the three of us. He actually *wanted* a tux. Says I'm killing a tradition with the suit idea." Riley waved a hand in dismissal. "I'm sure Ellie will talk some sense into him. That wife of his has been the best thing ever for ol' stick in the mud Finn."

Brody shook his head. "I can't believe you're talking about wedding plans. You've changed, little brother."

"For the better, believe me. Meeting Stace made me change everything about myself, my life. And I'm glad it did." The waitress came by their table to take their orders. Riley opted to try the new Autumn Lager, while Brody stuck to water.

Riley raised a hand when a few of their mutual friends came in. Then he turned back to Brody. "Want me to invite them over to join us?"

Brody thought of the small talk they'd exchange, idle chatter about women, work and sports. "I don't feel much like company. Maybe another time."

"You okay?"

"I'm fine." Brody pushed his menu to the side of the table and avoided his brother's gaze.

"Sure you are. Brody, you're still struggling. You should talk about it."

The waitress dropped off their drinks. Brody thanked her, then took a long sip of the icy water. Talking about it hadn't done any good. He'd lost patients before, back when he was an intern, and in the last few years, seen a few patients die of heart disease and cancer, but this one had been different. Maybe because he'd lacked the tools so easy to obtain here.

Either way, Brody didn't want to discuss the loss of Andrew. Of the three McKennas, Brody kept the most inside. Maybe it came from being the middle brother, sandwiched between practical Finn and boisterous Riley. Or maybe it stemmed from his job—the good doctor trying to keep emotion out of the equation and relying on logic to make decisions. Or maybe it stemmed from something deeper.

Admitting he had failed. Doctors were the ones people relied on to fix it, make it better, and Brody hadn't done either.

"By the way," Brody said, "if you guys don't have a cake picked out yet for the wedding, there's this bakery down the street from my office that does cupcake wedding cakes. They had a display in the window. I thought it looked kind of cool. I know you and Stace are doing the unconventional thing, so maybe this would be a good fit."

"Changing the subject again?"

Brody grinned. "Doing my best."

"Okay. I get the hint. No, we don't have a cake decided on yet. We planned this whole thing pretty fast, because all I want to do is wake up next to Stace every day of my life." Riley grinned, then narrowed his eyes.

"Hey, since when do you bring dessert to a get-together? Or heck, offer anything other than a reminder to get my flu shot?"

Brody scowled. "I thought it'd be nice for you and Stace."

Riley leaned forward, studying his older brother's face. "Wait…did you say bakery? Is it the one owned by that guy's sister?"

"Yeah." Brody shrugged, concentrated on drinking his water. "It is. But that's not—"

"Oh." Riley paused a second. "Okay. I get it. Good idea."

"I'm just offering to help defray the costs of your wedding."

"Whatever spin you want to put on it is fine with me." Riley chuckled. "Stace talked about baking the cake herself, but she's so busy with the diner, and then planning this thing. Let me talk to Stace and see if that works for her. I'll do that right now, in fact."

"You don't have to—"

"I don't mind, Brody. Not one bit." Riley's face filled with sympathy. Riley knew very little about Brody's time in Afghanistan. A few facts, but no real details, and only because Riley had brought over a six-pack of beer to welcome Brody home, and by the third one, Brody had started talking. He'd told Riley one of the military guys who had died had been local, that he'd struck up a friendship with the man before he died. But that was all. Brody had hoped broaching the subject would be cathartic. Instead, in the morning he had a hangover and ten times more regrets.

Riley flipped out his cell phone and dialed. "How's the prettiest bride in Boston today?"

Brody heard Stace laugh on the other end. He turned away, watched the hum of activity in the restaurant. Waitstaff bustling back and forth, the bartender joking with a few regulars, the tables filling and emptying like tidal pools.

"Stace loves the idea," Riley said, closing the phone and tucking it back into his pocket. "She said to tell you our colors are—"

"Your colors?" Brody chuckled. "You have a color scheme there, Riley?"

A flush filled his younger brother's cheeks. "Hey, if it makes Stace happy, it makes me happy. Anyway, go for bright pink and purple. Morning glories, you know?"

Brody nodded. His brother had told him about the meaning behind the diner Stace owned. The one started years before by her father, and decorated with the flowers that he had said reminded him of his daughter. A sentimental gift to a daughter he'd loved very much. "That'll be nice."

"Yeah," Riley said, as a quiet smile stole across his face, "it will."

How Brody envied his brother that smile. The peace in his features. The happiness he wore like a comfortable shirt.

It was the same thing Brody had been searching for, and not finding. He'd thought maybe if he stopped by and talked to Kate, made a step toward the promise he'd made, it would help. If anything, it had stirred a need in him to do more, to do…something.

Hence, the cupcakes. Now that he'd opened his big mouth, he'd need to go back there and place the order.

Damn.

"So how is work going?" Brody said before Riley turned the conversation around again. His brother had started an after school program at the arts centered high school he'd once attended. For creative, energetic Riley, the job fit well.

"Awesome. The kids at the Wilmont Academy are loving the program. So much, we opened it up to other kids in the area. We're already talking about expanding it in size and number of schools."

"That's great." The waitress brought their food and laid a steaming platter of mini burgers and fries in front of Riley, a Waldorf salad in front of Brody.

"Why do you eat that crap?" Brody said. "You know what it's doing to your arteries. With our family history—"

Riley put up a hand. "I love you, Brody, I really do, but if you say anything about my fries, I'm going to have to hurt you."

"I just worry about you."

"And I appreciate it. I'll do an extra mile on the treadmill tonight if that makes you feel better."

"It does. Did you get your flu—"

Riley tick-tocked a finger. "Don't go all doctor on me. I'm out to lunch with my brother, and we're talking about my job. Okay?"

Brody grinned. "Okay."

As if to add an exclamation point to the conversation, Riley popped a fry into his mouth. "Things at Wilmont, like I said, are going great. We've got classes in woodworking, dance, film, you name it. They're filling up fast."

"That's great."

"Oh, yeah, before I forget. We're having a career day

next month and we're looking for people to speak to the kids about their jobs. Answer questions about education requirements, things like that." Riley fiddled with a fry. "Maybe you could come in and do a little presentation on going into medicine. You know, a day in the life of a doctor, that kind of thing."

Brody pushed his salad to the side, his appetite gone. "I don't think I'm the best person to talk about that."

Riley's blue eyes met his brother's. Old school rock music flowed from the sound system with a deep bass and steady beat. "You're the perfect one. You've got a variety of experiences and—"

"Just drop it. Okay?" He let out a curse and shook his head. Why had he called his brother? Why had he thought it would make things better? Hell, it had done the opposite. "I just want to get you some damned cupcakes. How many do you need?"

Riley sighed. He looked like he wanted to say something more but didn't. "There should be fifty guests. So whatever it takes to feed that many. We're keeping it small. I figure I've lived enough of my life in the limelight. I want this to be special. Just me and Stace, or as close as we can get to that."

Brody nodded. Tried not to let his envy for Riley's happiness show. First Finn, now Riley, settled down and making families. For a long time, Brody had traveled along that path, too. He'd dated Melissa for a couple years, and he'd thought they'd get married. Then just before he took over Doc Watkin's practice, he'd spent two weeks working for free in a clinic in Alabama, tending to people who fell into the gap between insurance and state aid. He'd been in the middle of stitching up a kid with a gaping leg wound when Melissa had called to tell him she was done, and moving on.

"Thanks," Brody said, getting to his feet and tossing some money onto the table. He turned away, shrugged into his jacket. "I'll let the baker know about the cupcakes."

"Brod?"

Brody turned back. "Yeah?"

"How are you? Really?"

Brody thought of the physicals and sore throats and aches and pains waiting for him back in his office. The patients expecting him to fix them, make them better. For a month, in Afghanistan, he'd thought he was doing just that, making a difference, until—

Until he'd watched the light die in Andrew Spencer's eyes.

"I thought I was fine," Brody said. "But I was wrong."

CHAPTER THREE

KATE stared at the pile of orders on her desk, the paperwork waiting to be done, but found her mind wandering
to the handsome customer who had come in a couple
days ago. The doctor with the Red Sox basket, who
had been both friendly and...troubled. Yes, that was
the word for it. She'd joked with him about spreading
the word about the shop, told him it would be enough
to repay her work on the basket, and he'd said—

No it won't.

Such an odd comment to leave her with. What on
earth could he have meant? She hadn't done anything
more for him than she'd do for any other customer.
Changed a bow, added some feminine touches. It wasn't
like she'd handed over a kidney or anything. Maybe
she'd misheard him.

Kate gave up on the work and got to her feet, crossing to the window. She looked out over the alley that ran
between her shop and the one next door, then down toward the street, busy with cars passing in a blur as people headed home after work. The sound system played
music Kate didn't hear and the computer flashed mes-
sages of emails Kate didn't read.

Her mind strayed to Dr. Brody McKenna again. She

didn't know much about him, except that he was a Red Sox fan who'd been too distracted to notice the basket he'd picked out was more suited to a male than a female. Maybe he was one of those scattered professor types. Brilliant with medicine but clueless about real life.

She sighed, then turned away from the window. She had a hundred other priorities that didn't include daydreaming about a handsome doctor. She'd met two kinds of men in her life—lazy loafers who expected her to be their support system and driven career A-types who invested more in their jobs than their relationships.

Few heroes like Andrew, few men who lived every day with heart and passion. Until she met one like that, dating would run a distant second to a warm cup of coffee and a fresh from the oven cookie.

The shop door rang. Kate headed out front, working a smile to her face. It became a real smile when she saw her grandmother standing behind the counter, sneaking a red devil cupcake from under the glass dome. Kate put out her arms. "Grandma, what a nice surprise."

Nora laughed as she hugged her granddaughter. "It can't be that much of a surprise. I'm here almost every day for my sugar fix."

Kate released Grandma from the hug. "And I'm thrilled that you are."

Growing up, Kate had spent hours here after school, helping out in the shop and sneaking treats from under the very same glass dome. The sweet tooth came with the family dimples, she thought as she watched her grandmother peel the paper off the cupcake.

"Don't tell your grandfather I'm sneaking another cupcake," Nora warned, wagging a finger. "You know he thinks I'm already sweet enough."

"That's because he loves you."

Nora smiled at the mention of her husband. They had the kind of happy marriage so elusive to other people, and so valuable to those blessed with that gift. Unlike Kate's parents, who had turned fighting into a daily habit, Nora doted on her husband, always had, she said, and always would.

Nora popped a bite of cupcake in her mouth then looked around the shop. "How are things going here?"

"Busy."

"How's the hunt for a second location?"

Kate shrugged. "I haven't done much toward that yet."

"You had plans—"

"That was before, Grandma. Before..." She shook her head.

Nora laid a hand on Kate's shoulder. "I understand."

When Andrew had been alive, buying and opening new locations had been part of their business plan. But ever since he'd died, she'd had to work at keeping to that plan. Months ago, she'd found a spot for a second location in Weymouth, but had yet to visit it or run the numbers, all signs that she wasn't as enthused as she used to be.

Her grandmother smiled. "I like the idea of another Nora's Sweet Shop, but I worry about you, honey. If you want to take some time off, I'd be glad to step in and help. Your grandpa, too."

Kate looked at her eighty-three-year-old grandmother. She knew Nora would step in any time Kate asked her, but she wouldn't expect or ask that of Nora. "I know you would, and I appreciate that but I'm okay. You guys do enough for me making the daytime deliveries."

Nora waved that off. "It keeps us busy and gets us out of the house. You know we like tooling around town, stopping in to see the regular customers."

"You two deserve to enjoy your golden years, not spend them working over a hot oven. Besides, I'm doing fine, Grandma."

Nora brushed a strand of hair off Kate's face. "No you're not."

Kate nodded, then shook her head, and cursed the tears that rushed to her eyes. "I just…miss him."

She didn't add that she regretted, to the depth of her being, ever encouraging her brother to join the military. Maybe if she'd pushed him in another direction, or dismissed the idea of the military, he'd be here today.

Tears shimmered in Nora's eyes, too. She had doted on her grandson, and though she'd been proud of his military service, she had worried every minute of his deployment. "We all do. But he wouldn't want you to be sitting around, missing him. If there was one thing your brother did well, it was live his life. Remember the time he went parachuting off that mountain?"

Despite the tears, Kate smiled. Her brother had been a wild child, from the second he was born. He approached life head on—and never looked back. "And the time he skydived for the first time. Oh, and that crazy swim with the sharks trip he took." Kate shook her head. "He lived on the edge."

"While the rest of us stayed close to terra firma." Nora smiled. "But in the end, he always came back home."

"His heart was here."

"It was indeed," Nora said. "And he would want you to be happy, to celebrate your life, not bury it in work."

Before he left for Afghanistan, Andrew had tried to talk to her about the future. When he'd started on the what-ifs, she'd refused to listen, afraid of what might happen. Now, she regretted that choice. Maybe if she'd heard him out, she might have the secret to his risk taking. Something to urge her down the path they had planned for so long.

Andrew had soared the skies for the rest of them while the other Spencers offered caution, wisdom. She missed that about him, but knew she should also learn from him. Remember that life was short and to live every moment with gusto. Even if doing so seemed impossible some days. Kate swiped away the tears. "I'll try to remember that."

"Good." Nora patted her granddaughter on the shoulder. Then her gaze shifted to the picture window at the front of the shop. She nodded toward the door. "Ooh. Handsome man alert. Did you put on your lipstick?"

Kate laughed. Leave it to Nora to be sure her granddaughter was primped and ready should Mr. Right stride on by. Her grandmother lived in perpetual hope for great grandchildren that she could spoil ten times more than she'd spoiled her grandchildren. "Grandma, I'm not interested in dating right now."

"I think this guy will change your mind about that. Take a look."

The door opened and Brody McKenna strode inside. Kate's heart tripped a little. The doctor's piercing blue eyes zeroed in on hers, and the world dropped away.

She cleared her throat. "Back for another basket, Doctor?"

Way to go, Kate, establish it as a business only relationship. In the end, the best choice. Hadn't she watched her parents' marriage, started on a whim, with major differences in goals and values, disintegrate? She wanted a steady, dependable base, not a man who made her heart race and erased her common sense, regardless of the way Brody's lopsided smile and ocean blue eyes flipped a switch inside her.

"I just came by to thank you," he said. "The basket was a big hit. My grandmother sends her regards and her gratitude for the cherry chocolates. Especially those. In fact, I'm under strict orders to buy some more."

"Those are my favorites, too," Nora said. She leaned over the counter and put out a hand. "I'm Nora Spencer."

He smiled. "Ah, the famous Nora in Nora's Sweet Shop." He shook hands with her, and Kate swore she saw her eighty-three-year-old grandma blush. "Brody McKenna."

Nora arched a brow. "You're a *doctor,* you said?"

Kate wanted to elbow her grandmother but Nora had already stepped out of reach. Under the counter, she waved her hand, but Grandma ignored the hint.

"Yes, ma'am," Brody said. "I own a family practice right down the street from here. I took over for Doc Watkins."

"Oh, I remember him," Nora said. "Nice guy. Except for when he was losing at golf. Then he was grumpy. Every Wednesday, he played, so I learned never to make an appointment for first thing Thursday morning."

Brody chuckled. "Yep, you have him down to a tee."

Kate and her grandmother laughed at the pun. Then Nora tapped her chin, and studied Brody. "Wait... McKenna. Aren't you that doctor that volunteers all the time? Or something like that? I read about a charity your family heads up. Doctors and Borders or some-thing like that."

"Medicine Across Borders." He shifted from foot to foot. "Yes, I'm involved in that. We travel the coun-try and the world, providing volunteer medical help to people in need."

The name of the organization sounded familiar to Kate, but she figured maybe because she'd seen some-thing in the news about it. Brody McKenna, however, seemed unnerved by talking about the group. His gaze darted to the right, and his posture tensed. Maybe he was one of those men who didn't like his charity work to be a big deal. A behind the scenes kind of guy.

Nora leaned in closer to him. "So tell me, Doctor McKenna, is there a Mrs. Doctor?"

"Grandma," Kate hissed. "Stop that." Still, Kate checked his left hand. No ring. The doctor was a single man. And she didn't care. At all.

Uh-huh.

"No, ma'am, there isn't a Mrs. Doctor," Brody said. "But I am here about a wedding that's in the near future."

Disappointment filled Kate. She told herself to quit those thoughts. She'd seen the man once for a few min-utes and she didn't care if he married her next door neighbor or the Queen of England. For goodness sake, she'd turned into an emotional wreck today. And it was only Tuesday.

"I'd be glad to help you with that," she said, pull-ing out an order pad and a pen. "What do you need?"

"It's not for me. It's for my brother."

"Wonderful," Nora said. "In that case, we're even more glad to help you."

"Grandma, stop," Kate hissed again.

"It is nice to find such helpful and beautiful service in this city," Brody said with a smile.

Nora elbowed Kate. A little thrill ran through her at his words. Why did she care?

Darn those eyes of his.

"Oh, don't worry," Brody said. "I'm as far from getting married as a man can be. This is for my little brother, Riley. He's getting married next Saturday and it's a small, private affair, but I thought it would be nice to provide the dessert so his new bride doesn't have to cook it. She owns a diner in the city. Maybe you've heard of it. The Morning Glory."

"I've seen it before when I've been in the city," Kate said, stepping in with a change of subject before her grandmother found a way to turn a diner, a brother's wedding and a cupcake order into an opportunity for matchmaking. After all, hadn't Brody just said he had no interest in marriage? That screamed stay away, commitment-phobic bachelor. "Didn't the diner host an animal shelter thing a month ago?"

"It did. Went well. The diner's main chef is on a trip to Europe and they've got a new one filling in, but I think doing the dessert *and* the food might be a bit overwhelming for him. Plus it's a nice way for me to show my support for my brother and his new wife. As well as give some business to a local shop."

It all sounded plausible, but still, something about the story Brody told gave Kate pause. She couldn't put her finger on it. Why come here? To this shop? There were a hundred bakeries in the area, several dedicated to weddings. Why her shop?

She decided to stop looking a gift horse in the mouth.

She needed the income, and she'd be crazy to turn down the opportunity to get Nora's Sweet Shop name out there. Especially if she sthe tuck to the plan about expanding, every public event was an opportunity to spread the word, ease into new markets.

"You've come to the right place," Nora said, as if reading Kate's mind. "We've done lots of weddings."

"Yeah, I saw that cupcake thing you had in the window. My brother and his fiancé thought it'd be a great idea because they're having their wedding and reception at the diner. It's going to be more low-key than your traditional big cake and band kind of thing. They aren't your typical couple, either, and loved the idea of an atypical cake."

Kate thought a second while she tapped her pen on the order pad. "We could do a whole morning glory theme. Put faux flowers on top of the cupcakes and arrange them like a bouquet."

Brody nodded. "I like that. Great idea. And I know Stace—that's the bride—will love it, too. The diner is important to her."

The praise washed over Kate. She'd had dozens of customers rave about the shop's unique sweets. Why did this one man's—a stranger's—words affect her so? "How many people are we serving?"

"Uh, about fifty. I think that's what my brother said."

"Sounds great." She jotted some notes on the order pad, adding the details about the cupcakes, his name and the date of the event. Considering the number of orders already stacked up in her kitchen, adding his one into the mix would take some doing. Thank God she had her assistant Joanne to help. Joanne had the experience of ten bakers and had been with the shop for so many years, neither Kate or Nora could remember when she'd started.

"And what about a phone number?" Nora piped in. Kate shot her grandmother a glare, but Nora just smiled. "In case we need to get a hold of you."

Brody rattled off a number. "That's my office, which is where I usually am most days. Do you want my cell, too?"

"No," Kate said.

"Yes," Nora said. Louder.

Brody gave them the second number, then paused a second, like he wanted to say something else. He glanced across the room, at what, Kate wasn't sure. The cupcake display? The awards and accolades posted on the wall? "So, uh, thanks," he said, his attention swiveling back to her.

"You're welcome. And thank you for the order."

"You said spread the word." He shrugged and gave her a lopsided grin. "I did. I'm sorry it wasn't more."

She chuckled. "I appreciate all business that comes my way."

Again, he seemed to hesitate, but in the end, he just nodded toward her, said he'd call her if he thought of anything else, then headed out the door. Kate watched him go, even more intrigued than before. Why did this doctor keep her mind whirring?

"Why did you keep trying to fix us up?" Kate asked Nora when the door had shut behind Brody.

"Because he is a very handsome man and you are a very interested woman."

"I'm not at all."

"Coulda fooled me with those googly eyes."

Kate grabbed the order pad off the counter and

tucked the pen in her pocket. "My eyes are on one thing and one thing only. Keeping this shop running and sticking to the plan for expansion." Her gaze went to the article on the wall, the only one that truly mattered. To the plans she'd had, plans that seemed stalled on the ground, no matter how hard she tried to move them forward. "Because I promised I would."

Brody tried. He really did. He put in the hours, he smiled and joked, he filled out the charts, dispensed the prescriptions. But he still couldn't fit back into the shoes he'd left when he'd gone to Afghanistan. After all his other medical mission trips, he'd come back refreshed, ready to tackle his job with renewed enthusiasm. But not this time. And he knew why.

Because of Andrew Spencer.

Every day, Brody pulled the card out of his wallet, and kicked himself for not doing what he'd promised to do. Somehow, he had to find a way to start helping Kate Spencer. He'd seen the grief in her eyes, heard it in her voice. Andrew had asked Brody to make sure his sister moved on, followed her heart, and didn't let the loss of him weigh her down, and do it without telling her the truth. That he had been the one tending Andrew when he'd died.

She doesn't handle loss real well, Doc. She'll blame herself for encouraging me to go over here, and that'll just make her hurt more. Take care of her—

But don't tell her why you're doing it. I don't want her blaming herself or dwelling on the past. I want her eyes on the future. Encourage her to take a risk, to pursue her dreams. Don't let her spend one more second grieving or regretting.

When Brody had agreed, the promise had seemed easy. Check in on Kate Spencer, make sure she was okay, and maybe down the road, tell her about the incredible man her brother had been, and how Brody had known him. But now...

He couldn't seem to do any of the above.

Maybe if he wrote it down first, it would make the telling easier. He could take his time, find the words he needed.

The last patient of the day had left, as had Mrs. Maguire, and Brody sat in his office. His charts were done, which meant he could leave at any time. Head to his grandmother's for the weekly family dinner, or home to his empty apartment. Instead, he pulled out a sheet of blank paper, grabbed a pen, then propped the card up on his desk.

I never expected to bond with Andrew Spencer. To me, he was my guardian—and at times, a hindrance to the work I wanted to do, because he'd make me and the other doctors wait while he and his fellow troops cleared an area, double checked security, in short, protected our lives.

All I heard was a ticking clock of sick and dying people, but he was smarter than me, and reminded me time and again that if the doctors died, then the people surely would, too. That was Andrew Spencer—putting the good of all far ahead of the good of himself. He risked his life for us many times. But the last time—

Brody's cell rang, dancing across the oak surface of his desk. He considered letting it go to voicemail, but in the end answering the phone was easier than writing the letter. "Hello?"

"Dr. McKenna, this is Kate down at Nora's Sweet

Shop." Even over the phone, Kate's voice had the same
sweet tone as in person. Brody liked the sound of her
voice. Very much. Maybe too much. "I'm calling because there's a problem with your cupcake order. I...I
can't fill it. My assistant had to go out of town today
because her first grandchild came a little early, and that
leaves me short-handed with a whole lot of orders, not
to mention a huge one due tonight. Anyway, I took the
liberty of calling another bakery in town and they said
they'll be happy to take care of that for you. No extra
charge, and I assure you their work is as good as mine."

Kate Spencer was in a bind. He could hear the stress
in her voice, the tension stringing her words together.
He thought of that card in his pocket, and of the promise he'd made to Andrew to help Kate. Now, it turned
out that Brody's order had only added to her stress level.

"Anyway, let me give you the name and number of
the other bakery," she said. "They're expecting your
call, and have all my order notes."

Brody took down the number, jotting it on a Post-it
beside the letter he'd been working on. His gaze
skimmed the words he'd been writing again. *That was
Andrew Spencer—putting the good of all far ahead of
the good of himself.*

It was as if Andrew was nudging Brody from beyond
the grave. Do something, you fool. You said you would.
"Is there any way I can help?" Brody asked.

She laughed. "Unless you can come up with an experienced baker in thirty minutes who is free for the
next few days, then no. But don't worry, we'll be fine.
I do feel bad about the last minute notice on changing
suppliers, but I assure you the other bakery will do a

great job. Thanks again for the business, and please consider us in the future."

"In case I ever have another wedding to buy a cake for?"

"Well, you *are* a doctor," she said with a little laugh. "You know, most desirable kind of bachelor there is. God, I can't believe I said that. Something about being on the phone loosens my tongue to say stupid things." She exhaled. "I'm sorry."

"No, no, I'm flattered. Really. Most people who come to see me are complaining about something or other. It's nice to get a compliment once in a while."

She laughed again, a light lyrical sound that lit his heart. For the first time in days, it felt like sunshine had filled the room. "Well, good. I'm glad to brighten your day. Anyway, thanks again."

"Anytime." She was going to hang up, and his business with Kate Spencer would be through, unless he found a reason to buy a lot of chocolate filled baskets. He glanced again at the words on the page, but no brilliant way to keep her on the line came to mind.

"Thank you for understanding, Dr. McKenna." She said goodbye, then the connection ended. He stared at the phone and the number he'd written down for a long, long time. He read over his attempt at the letter, as half hearted as his attempts to keep his promise, then crumpled it into a ball and tossed it in the trash. Then he got his coat and headed out the door, walking fast.

Thirty minutes wasn't a lot of time to change a future, but Brody was sure going to try.

CHAPTER FOUR

WIND battered the small building and rain pattered against the windows of Nora's Sweet Shop. A fall storm, asserting its strength and warning of winter's imminent arrival. Kate sat at her desk, flipping through the thick stack of yellow order sheets.

She had two corporate orders. Three banquets. And now, the McKenna wedding—well, no, that one was safely in another bakery's hands. A lot of work for one bakery, never mind one person. On any other day, she'd be grateful for the influx of work. But today, it all just felt...overwhelming. She glanced over at the folder on her desk, filled with notes about expansions and new locations, then glanced away. That would have to be put on hold. For a long time.

Always before, baking had been her solace, the place where she could lose herself and find a sweet contentment that came from making something that would make people smile. But ever since Andrew's death, that passion for her job had wavered, disappearing from time to time like sunshine on a cloudy day.

Now, without her assistant on board, she knew getting the job done would take a Herculean effort. Best to just roll up her sleeves and get it done.

She glanced at the dark, angry sky. "I can't do this without you," she whispered to the storm above. Thunder rumbled disagreement. "We were supposed to expand this business together, take Nora's Sweet Shop to the masses. Remember? That's what you always said, Andrew. Now you're gone and I'm alone and trying like hell to stick to the plan. But…" she released a long, heavy sigh, "it's hard. So hard. I'm not the risk taker. I'm not the adventurer. You were. And now, the shop is in trouble and I…I need…help."

The bell over the door jingled. Kate jerked to her feet. For a second, she thought she'd round the corner and see Andrew, with his teasing grin and quick wit. Instead, she found the last answer she'd expect.

Brody McKenna.

He stomped off the rain on his shoes, swiped the worst of the wet from his hair, and offered her a sheepish smile, looking lost and sexy all at the same time. A part of her wanted to give him a good meal, a warm blanket, and a hug. She stopped that thought before it embedded itself in her mind. Dr. McKenna embodied dark, brooding, mysterious. A risk for a woman's heart if she'd ever seen one.

"Dr. McKenna, nice to see you again." She came out from behind the counter, cursing herself for smoothing at her hair and shirt as she did. "Did you have a problem with the other bakery?"

"No, no. I haven't even called them yet." He shifted his weight from foot to foot. The rain had darkened his lashes, and made his blue eyes seem even bluer. More like a tempestuous sea, rolling with secrets in its depths. "I, ah, stopped by to see if you had eaten."

She blinked. "If I had eaten?"

"I live near here and every night when I walk home, I see the light on." He took two steps closer. "Every morning when I leave for work, I see the light on in here." He took another two steps, then a few more, until he stood inches away from her, that deep blue ocean drawing her in, captivating her. "And it makes me wonder whether you ever go home or ever have time to have a decent meal."

"I…" She couldn't find a word to say. No one outside her immediate family had ever said anything like that to her. Worried that she'd eaten, worried that she worked too hard. Why did this man care? Was it just the doctor in him? Or something more? "I won't starve, believe me. I have a frozen meal in the back. I'll wolf it down between baking."

"That's not healthy."

She shrugged. "It's part of being a business owner. Take the bad with the good. And right now, the good is…well, a little harder to find." She didn't add that she planned on keeping herself busy in the kitchen because it kept her from thinking. From dwelling. From talking to people who were no longer here.

Brody leaned against the counter, his height giving him at least a foot's advantage over her. For a second, she wondered what it would be like to lean into that height, to put her head against his broad chest, to tell him her troubles and share her burdens.

Then she got a grip and shook her head. He was asking her about her eating habits, chiding her about working too much. Not offering to be her confidante. Or anything more.

"Listen, I eat alone way too often," he said. "Like

you, I work a lot more hours than I probably should and end up trading healthy food for fast food."

She laughed. "Doctor, heal thyself?"

"Yeah, something like that. So why don't we eat together, and then you can get back to baking or whatever it is you're doing here. It's a blustery night, the kind when you need a warm meal and some good company. Not something packaged and processed."

Damn, that sounded good. Tempting. Comforting. Perfect.

Despite her reservations, a smile stole across Kate's face. "And are you the good company?"

"That you'll have to decide for yourself." He grinned. "My head nurse thinks I'm a pain in the neck, but my grandmother sings my praises."

She laughed. "Isn't that what grandmothers are supposed to do?"

"I do believe that's Chapter One in the Good Grandma Handbook."

Kate laughed again. Her stomach let out a rumble at the thought of a real meal. Twice a week she went to Nora's for dinner, but the rest of her meals were consumed on the run. Quick bites between filling baking pans and spreading icing. Brody had a point about her diet being far from healthy. "Well, I am hungry."

"Me, too. And I don't know about you, but I...I don't want to eat alone tonight."

She thought of the gray sky, the stormy rumbles from the clouds and the conversations she'd had with her dead brother. "Me, either," Kate said softly.

Brody thumbed to the east. "There's a great little place down the street. The Cast Iron Skillet. Have you been there?"

The rumble in her stomach became a full-out roar. "I ate there a couple times after they first opened. They have an amazing cast iron chicken. Drizzled with garlic butter and served with mashed sweet potatoes. Okay, now I'm salivating."

"Then drool with me and let's get a table."

Drool with him? She was already drooling over him. Temptation coiled inside her. Damn those blue eyes of his.

She hesitated for a fraction of a second, then decided the work had waited this long, it could wait a little longer. She wasn't being much use in the kitchen right now anyway, and couldn't seem to get on track. Not to mention, she couldn't remember the last time she'd had a meal that hadn't come from the microwave. She grabbed her jacket and purse from under the counter, then her umbrella from the stand by the door. "Here," she said, handing it to him, "let's be smart before we go out in the rain."

But as Kate left the shop and turned the lock in the door, she had to wonder if letting the handsome doctor talk her into a dinner that sounded a lot like a date was smart. At all.

The food met its promise, but Brody didn't notice. He'd been captivated by Kate Spencer from the day he met her, and the more time he spent with her, the more intrigued he became. What had started as a way to get to know the person whom Andrew had raved about, the one who had written that card to her brother and sent Andrew so many care packages he'd joked he could have opened a store, had become something more. Something bigger.

Something Brody danced around in his mind but knew would lead to trouble. He was here to fulfill a promise, not fall for Andrew's sister.

Kate took a deep drink of her ice water then stretched her shoulders. She'd already devoured half her dinner, which told Brody he'd made the right decision in inviting her out. Like him, he suspected she spent more time worrying about others than about herself.

For the tenth time he wondered what had spurred him to invite her to dinner, when he'd gone over to the shop tonight to just check in on her, ask her how business was going, and somehow direct the conversation to expansions. Drop a few words in her ear about what a good idea that would be then be on his way, mission accomplished. Once again, his intentions and actions had gone in different directions. Maybe because he was having trouble seeing how to make those intentions work.

"I forgot…what kind of medicine do you practice?" she asked, as she forked up a bite of chicken. The restaurant's casual ambience, created by earth tone décor and cozy booths, had drawn dozens of couples and several families. The murmur of conversation rose and fell like a wave.

"Family practice," Brody said. "I see kids with runny noses. Parents with back aches. I've administered more flu shots than I can count, and taped up more sprained ankles than the folks at Ace bandage."

She laughed. "That must be rewarding."

"It is. I've gotten to know a lot of people over the years, their families, too, and it's nice to be a part of helping them live their lives to the fullest. When they take my advice, of course." He grinned.

"Stubborn patients who keep on eating fast food and surfing the sofa?"

He nodded. "All things in moderation, I tell them. Honestly, most of my job is just about…listening."

"How so?"

"Patients, by and large, know the right things to do. Sometimes, they just want someone to hear them say they're worried about the chances of having a heart attack, or scared about a cancer diagnosis. They want someone to—"

"Care."

"Exactly. And my job is to do that then try to fix whatever ails them." Which he'd done here, many times, but when it had counted—

He hadn't fixed Andrew, not at all. He'd done his best, and he'd failed.

"Where did you start out? I mean, residency." Kate's question drew Brody back to the present.

"Mass General's ER. That's a crazy job, especially in Boston. You never know what's going to come through the door. It was exciting and vibrant and…insane. At the end of the day, I could have slept for a week." He chuckled. "The total opposite of a family practice in a lot of ways. Not to say I don't have my share of emergencies, but it's less hectic. I have more time with my patients in family practice, which is nice."

"I have a cousin in Detroit who works in the ER. I don't think he's been off for a single holiday."

"That's life in the ER, that's for sure." Brody got a taste of that ER life every time he went on a medical mission trips and again in Afghanistan. "That's one of the perks Doc Watkins told me about when I took over the practice. There are days when all those runny noses can get a bit predictable, but by and large, I really enjoy my work."

"Same with cupcakes. Decorated one, decorated a thousand." She laughed. "Though I do like to experiment with different flavors and toppings. And the chocolates—those leave lots of room for creativity."

"Do you ever want to step out of the box, and do something totally different?"

"I have plans to." She fiddled with her fork. "My brother and I always wanted to expand Nora's Sweet Shop, to take it national, maybe even start franchising. Andrew was the one with the big, risky ideas. I'm a little more cautious, but when he talked, I signed on for the ride. He was so enthusiastic, that he got me excited about the idea, too."

"And have you expanded yet?" Brody crossed his hands in front of him, his dinner forgotten. Here was what he had come here to discuss, though he got the feeling it wasn't a subject Kate really liked visiting.

She shook her head. "I've thought about it. Even found a property in Weymouth that I saw online, but..." Kate sighed, "ever since Andrew died, it's been hard to get enthusiastic about the idea again. I know he'd want me to push forward but...it's hard."

Guilt weighed heavy on Brody's shoulders. Maybe if he'd been a better doctor, if he'd found a way to save Andrew, her brother would be here now, and Kate wouldn't be debating about opening another location. She'd be celebrating with Andrew.

Promise me.

Andrew had asked him to watch out for his little sister, to make sure she was moving on, living her life. Taking her to dinner was part of that, Brody supposed, but he knew Andrew had meant more than a platter of chicken Alfredo and some breadsticks.

"You should expand anyway. Your brother would want you to," Brody said, wondering if she knew how true that was. "And if it's a matter of financing, I can help if you want."

She laughed. "You? What do you know about franchising or opening new locations?"

"Uh...nothing. But I think it sounds like a great idea and if you need financial backing—" Was that what he was going to do? Throw money at the problem and send it away? "—then I am more than happy to provide that."

"You hardly know me. Why would you give me money, just like that? And how can you afford it?"

"I'm a McKenna, and part of being a McKenna means having money. I inherited quite a lot when my parents died, and my grandparents were good investors. Even after paying for medical school and my own practice, I've been left with more than I know what to do with." He leaned forward, wishing he had the magic words he needed. "I've tasted your cupcakes and chocolates. That's a business worth backing."

"Well, I appreciate the offer, but..."

"But what?"

"I'm not ready for expanding or any kind of a big change yet." She toyed with the fork some more. "Maybe down the road." She raised her gaze to his. Green eyes wide, looking to him for answers, support. "I think part of it is fear of the unknown, you know? Andrew was good at that, just leaping and looking afterwards. I'm one of those people who has to peek behind the curtains a few times before I do anything." She twirled some noodles onto her fork. "I'm the one in the back of the scenes, not out there leading the charge."

He watched her take a bite, swallow, then reach for her water. Every time he saw her, he saw the memory of her brother. They had similar coloring—dark brown hair, deep green eyes, high cheekbones. Andrew had been taller than Kate, tanned from his time in the desert. But Brody could still see so much of the brave young man in his younger sister.

A part of Brody wanted to leave, to head away from those reminders. To bury those days in Afghanistan and his regrets deep, so deep he would never remember them, never have them pop up and send him off-kilter again.

Except that would be the coward's way out, and Brody refused to take that path.

"I used to be that way, too," he said. "Afraid of the unknown. Then I went on my first medical mission trip, and it cured the scare in me."

"How?"

"You get dropped into a new place, with new people and new equipment, and you have to sink or swim. If you sink, then other people get hurt. So I had no choice but to buck up and get over my worries that I wouldn't be a good enough doctor."

But had he been a good enough doctor? Sure he'd helped people in Alabama, Alaska, Costa Rica, even here in Newton, MA, but when it came down to a moment that mattered, a moment when death waited outside the door, he hadn't been good enough after all. He had tried his best and he had failed.

Medical school had taught him over and over again that sometimes, people just die. Maybe that was true, or maybe it was just that the wrong doctor had been in charge that day. He had rethought every action of that day a hundred times, questioned every decision, and retraced his steps. But in the end, it didn't matter because no matter how much he did the day over in his head, it wouldn't bring Andrew back.

"I think just taking care of people like you do, and giving back on those trips you take, is brave enough," she said.

"I don't know about that. It's my job and I just try to do the best I can." Would he ever be brave enough to take on another mission? Or spend the rest of his life afraid of regretting his mistakes?

"My whole family has always been the kind that believes in giving to others," Kate said. "From bringing food to the shelters to donating to good causes, to giving people who need a second chance a job. That's easy, if you ask me. But doing what you do, going to a strange city or country and caring for people…that takes guts."

"There are others who do far gutsier jobs than I," he said. "They're the ones to admire, not me."

"I don't know. You've worked the ER at Mass General." She laughed. "That takes some courage, too."

He had no desire to sit here and discuss courage and himself in the same sentence. He'd come here to keep a promise, and knew he couldn't leave until he did. "Courage is also about going after your dreams, which is what I think you should do. Open that new location." He placed his hand on the table, so close he could have touched her with a breath of movement. "My offer to back you stands, so just know whenever you need me, I'll be there."

"You barely know me," she said again.

"What I know looks like a very good investment."

Her cheeks filled with pink, and she glanced away. "Well, thank you. I'll let you know if I move forward."

Damn. She didn't sound any more enthused about the idea now than she had before.

The other diners chatted and ate, filling the small restaurant with the music of clanking forks and clinking glasses. Waiters bustled to and fro, silent black clad shadows.

"I forgot to get more of those chocolates my grandmother wanted when I was at the shop the other day. She wanted me to also tell you that she liked those chocolate leaves you had in the basket," he said, keeping the topic neutral. Away from the hard stuff. "She said they were so realistic, she almost didn't want to eat them."

The pink in her cheeks deepened to red. "Thank you."

"Don't be embarrassed, Kate. It's clear you enjoy your work by how good the finished product turns out."

"I'm just not used to being the one in the spotlight. For years, I was the one in the back, baking. My grandmother was the face of Nora's for a long time, then Andrew and now…"

"You."

She smiled. "Me."

"You make a good face for the company. Sweet, like the baked treats." The words were out before he could stop them. Damn.

"Keep saying things like that, Dr. McKenna, and I'll never stop blushing." She grinned, then grabbed another breadstick from the basket.

"I wouldn't complain." What the hell was he doing? Flirting with her? He cleared his throat and got back to the reason for being here—a reason that eluded him more and more every minute. "It sounds like you enjoy your job a great deal."

"I do. Except when there's a huge stack of orders and I'm short on help. And…" She glanced at her watch. "Oh, darn, I almost forgot I have a delivery to make tonight." She pushed her plate to the side and got to her feet. "Thanks for dinner, but I have to go."

He rose and tossed some money onto the bill. "Let me walk you back."

She smiled. "It's only a couple blocks to the shop. I'm fine by myself."

"A gentleman never lets a lady walk home alone. My grandfather drilled that into me."

"A gentleman, huh?" The smile widened and her gaze assessed him. "Well, I wouldn't want you to disappoint your grandfather."

They headed out the door, back into the rain. Brody unfurled the umbrella over them, and matched his pace to Kate's fast walk. He noted the shadows under her eyes. From working hard, maybe too hard. She was doing exactly what Andrew had predicted—spending her days baking and wearing herself into the ground. Not taking care of herself. Hence the microwave dinners and shadows under her eyes. "Do you make many deliveries yourself?"

She shook her head. "My grandparents make the daytime deliveries—they enjoy getting out and seeing folks in the neighborhood, but they don't like to drive at night, so I handle those. I don't mind, but when I've been working all day…well, it can make for some long days."

"You need not one assistant, but a whole army of them."

She laughed. "I agree. And as soon as Joanne gets back and I have some time to run an ad and do some interviews, I'll be hiring, so I don't end up in this boat again."

They had reached the shop. Brody waited while she unlocked the door and let them inside. He set the wet umbrella by the door. Kate turned toward him. "Thanks for walking me back."

"No problem."

"And, I'm really sorry about having to send you to another bakery for the cupcake order. If there was a way to fit that in my schedule, believe me I would. I just had too many existing orders and not enough time." She grinned and put her hands up. "There's only one me."

"You could get a temp," he said. "I've hired them when my nurse is on vacation. And during busy seasons."

She waved that suggestion off. "Trying to find someone trained in cooking and willing to work just those few days…it's almost more work to do that than it is to just handle it myself. And right now, my time is so limited, I can't imagine adding to my To Do list."

She reminded Brody of himself when he had been an intern in medical school, burning the candle at both ends, and sometimes from the middle, too. "How are you going to get all the orders done? And make deliveries and do paperwork and all the stuff that goes with owning your own business?"

"Working hard. Working long hours. I do most of the baking after the shop closes, which means for very long nights sometimes." She shrugged. "I've done it before. I can do it again."

He saw the tension in her face, the shadows under her eyes, the weight of so much responsibility on her shoulders. Andrew had told him, in that long, long conversation that had lingered long into the night while Brody prayed and medicine failed, that his sister had poured her whole life into the shop, giving up dates, parties with friends, everything, to keep it running when the economy was down, and get it strong enough to take on the next challenge of expansion. Baking made her happy, especially during the tumultuous years of their childhood and after their parents' divorce, Andrew had said, and seeing his older sister happy had become Andrew's top mission. The business had meant as much to Andrew as it did to Kate. Andrew would never let it falter, even for a few days.

Nor would he want Brody to just keep throwing words at the problem. He had tasked Brody with making sure Kate moved forward, found that happiness again. That meant doing what Brody did best—digging in with both hands.

"What if I helped you?" Brody said.

"You?" She laughed as she crossed the room and flipped on a light. "Didn't you tell me you're all thumbs in the kitchen?"

"Well, yeah, but I can measure out doses." The urge to help her, to do something other than buy a damned basket of chocolates, washed over him in a wave. She wouldn't let him back her next location, and he didn't know enough to just go out there and buy one for her, but he could take up some of the slack for her. He followed her into the back room. "I'm sure I can measure flour and sugar and…whatever. And if I can take the temperature of a patient, I can add stuff to an oven. I may not have the best handwriting in the world—"

At that, she laughed.

"But I can handle putting some flowers on some cupcakes."

"I appreciate the offer, but I'm sure you're busy with your practice, and this would be a heck of a job to just jump into. I'll be fine." She had pulled a paper off the wall and read it over. The order that needed to be delivered, he surmised. At night, maybe to a less than desirable neighborhood, alone.

A thick stack of orders were tacked to the wall, waiting to be filled after she did this one. Piles of bakery supplies lined the far counter. Sacks of flour and sugar, tubs of something labeled fondant. A huge work load for anyone. Not to mention someone still reeling from a big personal loss.

Once again the urge to walk away, to distance himself from this reminder of his greatest mistake, roared inside him. If he did this, he'd be around Kate for hours at a time. At some point, the subject of her brother would come up. How long did he think he could go before the truth about why he was here came out?

Promise me.

Damned if he'd let her struggle here on her own. Andrew wouldn't want that.

Once she was stronger, ready for the rest, he would tell her how he had come to be in her shop that day. Andrew had warned Brody that his sister looked tough, a cover for a fragile heart, and cautioned him against telling Kate the truth. Brody suspected Andrew did on his deathbed what he'd done all his life—protected the sister he loved so much.

And now he'd given Brody that job. He'd deal with the rest when he had to, but for now, there was Kate and Kate needed help. He took a step closer. "Let me help you, at least with the delivery, and if we work well together, then maybe I can help you in here, too."

"I don't know. I—"

"It'll only be for a few days, you said so yourself. And I'll work for free. We can get that cupcake order done for my brother and I can be the hero of the wedding." He grinned. "Just let me help. I'll feel better if I do."

She leaned closer, her green eyes capturing his. "Why?"

"Because you need the help. And I...I need something to occupy my nights."

"Why?"

He could have thrown off some flippant answer. Something about being single and bored, or a workaholic who needed more to do, but instead, his gaze went to the far corner of the room, where a sister had pinned up an article about a brother who'd given his all, and the words came from deep in Brody's heart. Not the whole truth, but something far closer than he'd said up until now. "I'm working through some stuff. And I just need something to...take my mind off it, until I find the best way to handle it."

She worried her bottom lip, assessing him. "Okay, we'll start with the delivery. It's a simple one, just getting those cupcakes," she pointed to a stack of boxes on the counter, "over to a local place for a party they're having tonight."

"Okay." He hefted the boxes into his arms, careful to keep them level, then followed Kate out the back door and over to a van she had parked in the alley between her shop and the one next door. The words Nora's Sweet Shop reflected off the white panels in a bright pink script. Kate slid open the side door, and he loaded the boxes on racks inside the van.

She climbed into the driver's seat and waited for him to get in on the passenger's side. "Before we go, I better warn you, that this place can be a little...rowdy."

"Rowdy? In Newton?"

"Sort of. You'll see." She put the vehicle in gear, a bemused smile on her face. He liked her profile, the way the streetlights illuminated her delicate features.

They headed down the street, bumping over a few potholes. Kate drove with caution, keeping one eye on the road and one on the cargo in the back. He kept quiet, allowing her to concentrate on the still congested city roads. A few turns, and then they pulled into the parking lot of the Golden Ages Rest Home.

"A rowdy rest home?" He arched a brow.

She just grinned, then parked the van, got out and slid open the side door. "I hope you wore your dancing shoes."

"My what? Why?"

But Kate didn't explain. He grabbed several of the boxes and followed her into the building. Strains of perky jazz music filled the foyer. No Grandma's basement decorations here. The rest home sported cream and cranberry colored furnishings offset by a light oak wood floor and a chandelier that cast sparkling light over the space. A petite gray haired lady rushed forward when Kate entered. "I'm so glad you're here. The natives were getting restless." She placed a hand on Kate's arm. "Thank you so much for helping us out again. You are an angel."

Kate hefted the boxes. "An angel with dessert to the rescue! I'm always more than happy to help you all out, Mrs. White."

The older lady waved the last words off. "You know that calling me Mrs. White makes me feel as old as my grandmother. Call me Tabitha, Kate, and you'll keep me young at heart."

Kate laughed. "Of course, Tabitha. How could I forget that?"

"Maybe you're getting a little old, too, my dear," Tabitha said, with a grin. She beckoned them to follow. They headed down the hall and into a room decked out for a party.

A pulsing disco ball hung from the ceiling, casting the darkened room in a rainbow of lights. Couches had been pushed against the walls, but few people sat on them. Jazz music pulsed from the sound system, while couples and groups of seniors danced to the tunes, some on their own, some using walkers and canes as partners. On the far wall, sat a table laden with food and drinks, and a wide open space waiting for dessert.

A tall elderly man with a full head of thick white hair and twinkling blue eyes, came up to Kate as soon as she entered the room. "Miss Kate, are you here to give me that promised dance?"

"Of course, Mr. Roberts." She rose to her toes and bussed a kiss onto his cheek. "Let me get dessert set up and I'll be ready to tango."

"Glad to hear it. Oh, and I see you brought a partner for Mrs. Williams." The man nodded toward Brody. "I didn't know you had another brother."

"Oh, he's not my brother."

"A beau?" Mr. Roberts grinned and shot a wink at Brody. "That's wonderful, Miss Kate. You deserve a man who will treat you right." He eyed Brody. "You *are* going to treat her right, aren't you?"

Brody sputtered for an answer, but Kate saved him by putting a hand between the men. "Oh, no, Brody's not a beau. Just a…friend."

Friend. The kiss of death between a man and a woman, Brody thought. But really, did he want anything more? Brody wanted to help Kate, not be her boyfriend.

Yet the thought of them having nothing more than a cordial relationship left him with a sense of disappointment. A war between what he wanted and what he should have brewed in his chest. He opted for the should have. Help her through this bump in her business, make sure she got back on track, that she was happy and secure again, then go back to his life. No more. No less.

"What, are you nuts, boy? This woman is a catch and a half. If I was thirty, okay," Mr. Roberts winked, "fifty years younger, I'd marry her myself."

"Mr. Roberts, you are an incorrigible flirt."

"Keeps me young." He grinned. "And keeps the ladies around here on their toes."

"Speaking of people on their toes," Kate said, "I better get dessert on the table before dinner is served."

She and Brody headed across the room, and started loading the cupcakes onto the waiting trays. A flock of eager and hungry partygoers lingered to the side, waiting for them to finish. Several people greeted Kate by name, and raved about her cupcakes. When she and

Brody were done, they stowed the empty boxes under the table, and stepped to the side.

"Tabitha wasn't kidding." Brody glanced around the room. "People are dying for those cupcakes. I think if we waited any longer, you'd have had a riot on your hands."

Kate laughed. "It's that way every month. I donate dessert for the Senior Shindig, and people are always already lined up to get one, sometimes before I even get here."

"That's because everyone here loves your desserts, and you," Brody said.

She brushed the bangs off her forehead and watched the residents shimmy to a fifties be-bop tune. "This place has always had a tender spot in my heart. Bringing the dessert for their events has sort of become a family tradition. When Andrew and I were kids, my grandparents used to bake for them. My great grandparents, Nora's parents, lived here, and from the beginning, the shop donated treats. On the weekends, Andrew and I would help deliver the cupcakes. The residents got to know us and we got to know them. We've cried when people have passed away, celebrated when they hit milestones, and helped them weather storms whenever we could."

"Weather storms?"

She leaned against the wall, while her gaze scanned the room. "This place was started by a husband and wife team who wanted to provide a low-cost but really nice option for retirees who needed a caring place to live. Because of that, it's faced some financial challenges, so my brother and I followed in my grandparent's footsteps, and over the years, we donated our time and talents to help them out. As a result, a lot of these residents are…well, friends. Sort of an extended family."

All in keeping with the jovial, caring hero that Brody had met in Afghanistan. A young man who would put his life in front of another's without thinking twice. Kate possessed those same admirable traits. Brody's esteem for her rose several notches, and so, too, did his connection with her. He could see some of the same spirit that had driven him into medicine, shining in her eyes as she took in the room. Kate was what Brody's grandmother would call a "good soul," the kind of woman who put others ahead of herself. "So you're not just the baker, but the dance partner as well?"

She laughed. "I like coming here. The residents remind me of what's important and what I get to look forward to."

"You're looking forward to the days of walkers and canes and wheelchairs?"

"In a way, yes. I mean, look at them." She waved toward the people around them. "These truly are their golden years. These are people who are happy and content with who they are. They've achieved their goals, realized their dreams, for the most part, and now they want to enjoy their lives. If a red devil cupcake can help in that a little bit, I'm more than happy to bake a few dozen."

"But doesn't that put you behind on your other work?"

"Some work," Kate said, her voice soft while she watched the crowd of people move about the room, "pays so much more than money. That's what Andrew always said, and it's true."

"I agree." Brody watched the happy faces of the residents as they greeted Kate, complimented the cupcakes. "That's how I feel about working in medicine. It's not about the money—and the medical mission work is all volunteer, so there's no money there at all, it's about the return on my time. The satisfaction at the end of the day is—"

"Priceless." She turned to him and smiled. "Then that's something we have in common."

He could feel the thread extending in the space between them, interlocking him more and more every minute with Kate Spencer. "It is indeed."

They were bonding, he realized, doing the very thing he had told himself not to do. But a part of Brody couldn't resist this intriguing woman who blushed at compliments and gave of her heart to so many around her.

Mr. Roberts stepped up to Kate and put out his arm. Just as she put her hand on the older man's arm, the perky elderly woman who had greeted them at the door sidled up to Brody. "Care to dance, young man? I hope you know the foxtrot."

"Be careful." Kate laid a hand on Brody's. "Tabitha can cut a rug better than Ginger Rogers."

"Now don't say that, Kate," the other lady said. "You'll scare off my dancing partner."

"I'm not much of a dancer." Brody offered up a sheepish grin. "That's my brother Riley's department."

"You're young and you have your original hips," Tabitha said. "That's good enough for me. Come on, honey, let's show those young kids we can outdance them." She took his hand and led him to the floor, followed by Kate and Mr. Roberts. The music shifted to a slow paced waltz, and Brody put out a hand and an arm to Tabitha. The older lady slipped into the space with a very young giggle, and they were off, stepping around the room with ease.

He tried to keep his attention on the chatty woman in his arms, but Brody's gaze kept straying to Kate. She laughed at something Mr. Roberts said, her head thrown back, that wild mane of rich dark brown hair cascading down her shoulders, swinging across his back, begging to be touched. Her lithe body swung from step to step, a sure sign she'd danced dozens of times before. As she danced a circle with Mr. Roberts, the people in the room said hello, thanked her for the cupcakes, and each one received a kind word or a friendly smile in return.

Too often, Brody had seen business people who cared about dollars and cents, not about people. Kate had that unique combination of heart and grace, coupled with killer baking skills. He admired that about her. He admired a lot about her, in fact.

Mr. Roberts swung Kate over to the space beside Brody, then sent a wink Tabitha's way. "Hey, Tabby, isn't it partner *change* time?"

"Partner change time?" The other woman gave him a blank look, paused, then a slow, knowing nod. "Oh, yes, of course. Partner change time. Thanks for the dance, kiddo." She stepped out of Brody's arms and into Mr. Roberts's, leaving Kate standing on the floor.

She laughed and watched the older couple spin away. "Not exactly subtle, are they?"

"About as subtle as a bull horn." Until that moment, Brody hadn't realized how much he had been waiting for an opportunity to dance with Kate. To feel her in his arms, instead of watching her in another's. This woman had intrigued him, captivated him, and even as he told himself this was a *bad idea* on a hundred levels, he put out his arms. "Shall we, partner?"

"I think we shall." She stepped into the circle created by his embrace, and they began to move together to the music. The big band sounds swirled in the air around them, as other couples whooshed back and forth in a flurry of colors and low conversations.

As they danced, the other people in the room disappeared, the lights narrowed their focus, and every ounce of Kate's attention honed in on Brody. She could have been dancing on the moon and wouldn't have noticed a thirty-foot crater underfoot. Her heart beat in rhythm with the steps, and her body tuned to his hand pressed to the small of her back, the warmth of his palm against hers, the way his dark woodsy cologne wrapped around them in a tempting cloud. She could see the slight five o'clock shadow on his chin, watch the movement of his lips with each breath, and she wondered how it would feel if he kissed her.

Working through some stuff.

That was what he had given as his reason for wanting to help her. Kate wanted to ask, to probe, to find out what had caused the shadows in his eyes. What he wasn't telling her—and what had been in all those odd comments that he'd never explained. But Kate Simpson didn't want anyone asking about the shadows in her own eyes, so she sure as heck wasn't going to ask about his.

And that meant not letting one dance distract her, or wrap her in a spell. She'd stick to business only. Period.

"Thank you again for dinner and for helping me with the delivery tonight," she said.

"I wasn't a bad cupcake transporter?" he asked as he turned her to the right, exerting a slight bit of pressure to help her move. How she wanted to lean into that touch, but she didn't.

She knew better than to try to step up and solve another man's problems. To be the shoulder he cried on, the heart he leaned on, only to leave her alone in the end when he returned to his busy life. How many times had she seen her mother crying, alone? How many times had she heard their fights, watched the destruction of their marriage a little at a time? She'd come close herself to repeating that mistake with her last boyfriend, and had no intentions of doing that again.

"Not bad at all," she said.

"Thanks." He chuckled. "It's always nice to have a back up career, should there ever be a sudden need for cupcake transportation throughout the greater Massachusetts area."

She laughed. The song had come to an end, and they broke apart, and made their way to where the parquet met carpet, carving out a corner of the room for themselves, apart from the others. Despite her reservations, and her determination to keep things platonic, she liked Brody. Liked spending time with him. He had a wit that could coax a laugh out of her on her worst day, a smile that made her forget her stress, and eyes that inspired all kind of other thoughts that had nothing to do with work.

It might not be so bad to have him around, particularly when the days got long and her thoughts drifted toward Andrew, and she found herself ready to cry. Her brother, she knew, wouldn't want her to do that, but getting past the loss was far from easy.

Easier, though, when Brody was around, she'd found. Maybe it wouldn't be so bad to have him in her kitchen for a time. "If you want to learn the baking business,

I'd be a fool to turn down free help. Especially sort of experienced free help."

Brody nodded toward Mr. Roberts and Tabitha, who were watching from the sidelines. Tabitha sent up a little wave. "I do come with the recommendations of Tabitha. Wait, that was just for my dancing skills. Is there a lot of call for dancing in your bakery?"

"Not so much, but I'm sure we can figure something out." She put out her hand. "Just remember—in the cupcake operating room, I'm the one in charge."

"Yes, ma'am." He grinned, then took her hand and when they shook, the warm connection sent a tremor through Kate's veins.

She dropped his hand and vowed that no matter what, the only thing she'd be cooking up in her kitchen over the next few days was dessert. Not a relationship with a handsome doctor. She could see in his eyes, in those shadows and in his soft words, that he needed someone.

And the one thing Kate vowed never to be again was the kind of person who filled that gap. To be a temporary pillow before the man returned to his driven life and discarded her like a forgotten towel on the floor. Because her heart was already scarred and one more blow would surely damage it forever.

CHAPTER FIVE

THE logistics of Brody's plan required more finesse than negotiating a peace treaty. A busy family practice doctor couldn't just up and walk out of the office to bake cupcakes. He'd told Mrs. Maguire he needed a bit of breathing room. "Just to get back into the swing of things," he'd said. "It's been a big change coming back from being overseas."

She'd put a hand on his shoulder, her brown eyes filled with kindness. "I understand. You take care of you and I'll take care of the schedule."

In a matter of hours, she'd managed to free half his days for the coming week. Brody made a mental note to send Mrs. Maguire a big box of chocolates and a gift certificate to her favorite restaurant. Maybe two gift certificates.

The day brightened as the sun began its journey to the other side of the sky. Odd how the same sun that warmed Boston's streets created an oven in Afghanistan. And how the same sun that shone over a quiet neighborhood street could shine over a war zone peppered with the wounded and the dead.

The dead—like Andrew Spencer. Cut down before he'd lived a fraction of his life.

Guilt washed over Brody, teemed in his chest. He'd done all he could, but still, it never seemed he'd done enough. Had he missed something? Forgotten something? Taken too few risks—

Or too many?

The what ifs had plagued Brody ever since Andrew's last stuttering breath. They'd been a heavy blanket on his shoulders as he'd boarded a plane to return to his family, knowing another plane had brought Andrew home to his family, stowed in a wooden casket in the cargo hold.

He could still see Andrew's wide green eyes, trusting Brody, hoping that Brody would pull off an eleventh hour miracle. Then trust had given way to fear, as the reality hit home. All the while, Brody battled death, tending to Andrew, then to the other wounded soldiers, assessing wounds based on survivability, and making his priorities off that grim reality.

Those who would die no matter what were put to the end of the list. While those who had a chance were helped first. Brody and the other doctor with him had worked on the others, knowing Andrew's chances...

Brody cursed as he drew up short outside the cupcake shop. Why had he agreed to do this? And why would Andrew pick him, the doctor who had tended him until his last breath, to watch over Kate? The task loomed like a mountain, impossible.

Inside the building, Kate crossed into his line of vision. She saw him outside and shot him a wave. Today, she had her hair up in a clip that poufed the back in a riot of curls. The style accented her delicate features, drew attention to her emerald eyes.

Maybe not impossible, just tough as hell. As he

watched Kate, he decided no matter what mountain faced him, it would be worth the climb.

Brody opened the door and stepped inside. Sweet scents of vanilla, chocolate, berry, wrapped around him like a calorie laden blanket. "Damn, it smells good in here."

"Thanks." Kate smiled. "If you ask me, it smells like temptation on a stick. Working here makes staying on any kind of diet impossible."

His gaze traveled over her lithe frame. She had on a V-necked black T-shirt emblazoned with the shop's logo and a pair of body hugging jeans. Tempting was exactly the word he'd use, too. "I'd say you're doing just fine in that department."

Had he just flirted with her? What the hell was he thinking?

A pale pink flush filled her cheeks, and the smile widened. "Well, thank you again." Her eyes lit with a tease. She wagged a finger at him. "But don't think you're getting out of dishes just because you complimented me."

"Damn," Brody said, then grinned. "And here I thought you'd go easy on me."

"And why would I do that?"

"Because of my charming good looks and great bedside manner, of course."

She laughed. "That might work with the nurses, but I'll have you know, I am a tough taskmaster."

He closed the gap between them, and his gaze dropped to her lips. Desire warred with his common sense. "How tough?"

"Very." She took a breath, and her chest rose, fell. "Very tough."

The urge to kiss her roared inside him. If there was one woman on this planet Brody shouldn't date, it was her. Already, he'd gotten too close, gotten too involved, when he had promised to help her, not fall for her.

Damn. Holding back the truth only made it worse. Everything in Brody, all the practical, logical, deal with the facts sides of him, wanted to tell Kate who he was. But Andrew had been firm—

Don't tell her. I don't want her to dwell on what happened to me or to blame herself for suggesting I enlist. I want her to move forward.

Telling her, Andrew had said, would leave Kate hurting, in pain again. That was the last thing Brody wanted to bring to Kate Spencer's life—more hurt and pain. He was here to make her laugh, not cry.

"Here." Kate thrust a bright pink apron between them. "Sorry I don't have any in more manly colors."

"This'll be fine." He slipped it over his head. "Reminds me of med school when one of my roommates did the laundry one week and washed the lab coats with a red sweatshirt. We were all pink for a while."

Kate laughed. "My brother said the pink made him look approachable to the ladies."

"I'll keep that in mind."

"Though, I have to say, Andrew was one of the most manly men I've ever known. When the war started, he told me he wanted to make a difference. So I said he should..." She shook her head and her eyes misted. "He joined the National Guard, and really took to the job. Everything Andrew did, he gave a hundred and ten percent."

Brody swallowed hard. "I'm sorry for your loss."

Such inadequate words. He'd said them many times

over the years of being a doctor, but never had they run more hollow than right now. Maybe because he knew Andrew, and knew that loss didn't even begin to describe the hole now left in the world.

"It's okay. I've always wondered and wished..." She shook her head again and bit her lip. "Anyway, he died doing what he loved. And although I miss him every single day, I'm proud of him." She swiped at her eyes, and let out a long breath. "Now let's to get to work so he can be proud of me, too."

Brody followed her into the kitchen in the back. Stainless steel countertops and machines gleamed under the bright lights. Here, the sweet scents were stronger, a tempting perfume filling the space. "So, where do we start? With Riley and Stace's cupcakes?"

"Not yet. We'll be making those closer to the date of the wedding, so they'll be fresh. Right now, we have another cupcake order to complete." She pointed to a huge sack on the floor. "You offered to be the muscle, so let's see how much muscle you have. I need five pounds in that mixer there."

He lifted the heavy bag, then gave her a blank look. "Do I just dump the whole thing in?"

She laughed. "No. Weigh it in that container on the scale, then when I tell you, you're going to add it, a little at a time." She dropped sticks of butter into the mixing bowl, then added sugar and turned on the beaters. "Have you ever cooked anything before?"

"Does making grilled cheese with an iron count?" He grinned. "Old college trick. Some wax paper from a cereal box, a loaf of bread, a package of cheese and an iron, and dinner is done."

"All I can say is thank God you went into medicine

instead of the restaurant industry." She added eggs, one at a time, keeping the beaters whirring until the mixture blended into a pale yellow ribbon. She crossed to Brody and added the rest of the dry ingredients to the flour. "Now remember, add a little at a time, otherwise the flour will go everywhere and we'll get covered. I'm baking cupcakes, not you and me."

Heat flushed her face. What was that? You and me? *Focus, Kate, focus.*

So she did, concentrating on the recipe instead of on Brody McKenna. And the reasons why he was here. Why he had cut his schedule in half to help her. And why work with her, of all the people in the city of Boston?

A few minutes later, the two of them scooped the batter into cupcake liners, then popped the trays into the oven. Kate started melting some chocolate, then laying out molds for the candy orders. "We'll pour these, then make the pink flowers that go with them. By then the cupcakes should be cooled and ready to frost. If you want to start the buttercream frosting, I'll get the ingredients out for you. Frosting is pretty simple. Dump and mix."

"That I can handle." He shot her a lopsided grin, then he paused and stepped forward. The streetlights glimmered outside, casting a golden glow over the counter under the window. The city's busy hum had dropped to a whisper. The storm had broken, and from time to time, a night bird called out.

Kate's gaze met Brody's. He had the bluest eyes she'd ever seen. A color as rich and true as the ocean. Eyes that studied her and analyzed her, and made her heart trip.

What the heck was she doing here?

Because right now it didn't feel like baking cupcakes. At all.

"You're good at this," he said.

"Thanks."

"I can make a huge mess just heating up restaurant takeout. But you…" he gestured toward the kitchen counters, "you manage to keep this place clean from start to finish."

The flush returned to her cheeks. "Oh, I'm not that neat. You should see my bookshelves and my closets." Had she just invited him to her apartment? If she danced any closer to the edge, she'd fall over—and fall for Mr. Wrong. She wanted steady, dependable, quiet, not a man who turned her insides into Jell-o and sent a riot of desire roaring through her whenever he smiled.

"I didn't say you were that neat," he said, and the grin played again on his lips, "because you, uh, have some flour…"

He reached out a finger, slid it down her cheek. A warm, slight touch. Sexy in its innocence. She drew in a breath, held it. "Right there," he finished.

"Thank you." The words were a whisper. Her heart hammered in her chest.

"Anytime." His voice dropped, low, husky, tempting.

His hand lingered against her cheek for a long, dark second. Was he going to kiss her? Did she want him to?

Then the oven timer beeped and broke the spell. She stepped back. "We…we should get back to work."

"Yeah." Those blue eyes locked on hers. "We wouldn't want anything to get burned."

"No. We wouldn't." She grabbed a pair of potholders and turned toward the oven before she could question whether he was talking about cupcakes—or them. She opened the oven, took out the trays and laid them on the counter to cool for a minute before she could remove the cupcakes and set them on racks.

Brody stood to the side, watching her. "You go a million miles a minute here. No wonder you never have time to eat."

"There are days when it's slow." Then she looked at the list of orders clipped to the board against the wall and laughed. "Though I have to admit, there aren't too many of those. Thank goodness."

"Admit it. You're just as Type A as I am."

She bristled. "I'm as far from Type A as you get."

"You run your own business, work too many hours, dig in and get the work done regardless of the obstacles in your way." He flicked out fingers to emphasize his list. "That defines Type A to me."

"You've got me all wrong." She turned away, and started taking the cupcakes out of the pans. Just as she'd thought. He'd admitted he was the exact kind of career focused man she tried to avoid. The kind who swept a woman off her feet, then left her in the dust when his job called. "My father was type A-plus. He worked every second he could. Took on extra shifts because he was convinced no other surgeon could do as good a job as he could."

"Your father was a doctor, too?"

"Yes. So that means I know the type. Come home at the end of the day, dump an emotional load on the family dinner table, then leave again when it's time for play practice or violin lessons. That is *not* me." How could he see her in that same light? She had a life, a world outside this bakery. Her gaze dropped to the cupcakes before her. Didn't she? "At all."

"Not all doctors are the same. And even so, being driven isn't always a bad thing, you know," he said. "That's the kind of trait that encourages you to do things like expand the business, open new locations."

"You're here to help, Dr. McKenna, not analyze me or my life choices." Suddenly he seemed much closer than when he'd been touching her a moment ago. She didn't need anyone to hold a magnifying glass to her life, or her choices. Because when they did that, all she could see was mistakes. "I'd appreciate it if you stuck to mixing dough and left the personal issues to the side. You stay out of my personal life and I'll stay out of yours. I'm sure you don't want me analyzing why you're working here instead of taking care of patients."

He stared at her for a long moment. His jaw worked, then he let out a long breath. "Yeah, I agree. Keeping this impersonal is best for both of us."

"Agreed." She should have been relieved that he agreed. Then why did a stone of disappointment weigh on her chest? She stowed the baked cupcakes in the refrigerator then removed her apron and laid it over a chair. "We're done here tonight."

"Yeah," he said quietly. "We are."

That couldn't have gone worse if he'd lit a flame to the night and set it ablaze. Regret filled Brody the next morning, heavy and thick. He sat in a booth at the Morning Glory, thinking for a man intending to do the right thing, he kept going in the wrong direction.

"Hey, Brody, how you doing?" Stace plopped a coffee cup before him and filled it to the brim with steaming java.

"Great, now that I have some coffee." He grinned. "How about you? Getting nervous about the wedding?"

She cast a glance toward Riley across the room, talking to one of the other customers. Riley caught his fiancé looking at him and gave her a wide smile. "How can I be nervous when I'm marrying the man of my dreams?"

Jealousy flickered in Brody. Finn had Ellie, and wore the same goofy smile as Riley every day. His two brothers had found that elusive gift of true love. To Brody, a man who measured everything in doses and scientific facts, it seemed an anomaly worthy of Haley's Comet.

The door to the diner opened, and instead of his older brother striding in, as Brody had expected, his grandmother entered. Stace went over and greeted her, followed by Riley. Mary said hello, then headed straight for Brody's table.

Mary McKenna wasn't the kind of woman to make social calls. Even as she eased out of her position at the helm of McKenna Media and groomed her grandnephew Alec to take the top spot, she spent her days with purpose. There were lists and appointments, tasks and goals. So when she slid into the seat opposite him, he knew she hadn't come by to chit-chat.

"Gran, nice to see you." He rose, and pressed a kiss to her cheek.

"Brody. I missed you at dinner the other night." It was an admonishment more than anything else. His seventy-eight-year-old grandmother, Brody knew, worried about him, and that meant she liked to see him regularly so she could be sure he wasn't wallowing away in a dark corner.

"Working late. Sorry."

"Working late…baking?"

"How'd you know that's where I was?"

"Your brothers are worse than magpies, the way they talk." A smile crossed her face. "Riley said you missed your regular lunch with him and when he asked Mrs. Maguire where you were, she said you were making cupcakes. He told Finn, and Finn told me."

His brothers. He should have known. Finn and Riley had found their happily ever afters and seemed to be on a two-man mission to make sure Brody did the same. They'd done everything short of bring him on a blind date shotgun wedding. Brody rolled his eyes. "I wish my brothers would stay out of my life."

"They only interfere because they love you." She pressed a hand to his cheek. "And so do I."

His grandmother had been a second mother to him for so long, there were days it seemed like it had always been just his grandparents and the McKenna boys. They'd been a rock in a turbulent childhood for all three boys, and stayed that way long after the McKennas graduated college, moved out on their own and became adults. After her husband's death three years ago, Mary had taken over the full time running of McKenna Media, but still doted on her grandsons with a firm but loving touch.

Brody's gaze softened, and he covered his grandmother's hand with his own. "I love you, too, Gran."

"And thank you for following up with my doctor this morning. You know you don't have to do that."

"I just worry about you, Gran. Wanted to make sure he covered all the bases."

"You do enough worrying for five doctors." She gave

his hand a squeeze. "I'm fine. Just suffering from a little old age."

He chuckled. "Glad to hear it."

Stace brought over a cup. "Some coffee, Mrs. M?"

"Goodness, no, dear. I'll slosh out of here if I drink any more." She pressed a hand to the belly of her pale gray suit. "But thank you."

"No problem. Let me know if you want to order anything." Stace headed off to another table.

"I like that girl," Mary said. "Sassy, strong, smart, and most of all, perfect for Riley." She returned her attention to Brody. "I just suffered through a long, excruciating meeting with the head of Medicine Across Borders. That's why I came by today. Finn is meeting me here in a second, so we can chat about the group."

His eldest brother had become more involved with the McKenna Foundation's overseas mission work after he'd married Ellie and adopted Jiao, an orphan from China. He'd been instrumental in organizing fundraisers and getting the word out.

"Was Larry at the meeting?" Brody asked. The assistant director had gone on his own mission a few weeks prior. Brody had always liked the older man, who had dedicated his life to the charity. Both Brody and Larry had a special place in their hearts for Medicine Across Borders because it took what he and other doctors did in the United States and multiplied it around the world.

"No, he's still in Haiti. It's been rough, he said." Gran sighed. "He lost a few patients last week. One of them a child, and it hit him hard. He said he wished that you were there because you're the best doctor he knows."

Brody shook his head. "Larry doesn't need me."

"I don't know about that," Gran said. "Larry talked to

me about that time you worked that clinic in Alabama. He said you changed those people's lives. They raised enough money to hire a second doctor after you left, and the mortality rate there has dropped significantly, in part because of those diabetes and heart disease awareness programs you started."

"I just did my job."

"You don't give yourself enough credit," Gran said. "You always were the one who worried too much and made it your personal mission to fix everything. Ah, Brody, you don't have to take so much on your shoulders."

"I'm not doing that, Gran."

"You do it and you don't even realize it. You protect the family, you protect your patients, and I suspect you're even protecting that pretty bakery owner. Sometimes, people have to face their worst fears and face the worst possible outcome in order to learn and grow. Protecting them can do them a disservice." She read his face, and let out a sigh. "You disagree, but maybe you'll think about it. Anyway, Larry said to say hello to you. He should be home in about a month. He says there's still a lot of need for basic medical care in Haiti, but he's making a dent, one patient at a time."

Brody listened to his grandmother's news about the charity, but his mind kept drifting to Kate Spencer. He had dodged her question, and dodged an opportunity to tell her the truth. Why?

He knew why. Because he was starting to like her. As much as he'd told himself he had no right to get involved with her, and no room in his life for a relationship right now, he had started to fall for her. She was sweet and funny and despite everything, upbeat and cheery. She was like a daisy in the middle of a lawn that had filled with weeds.

And if he told her—

It would devastate her. She'd relive her brother's death, hold herself responsible for him being there.

Maybe his grandmother had a point. Maybe in protecting her, he was hurting her more.

"Brody? Did you hear me?" his grandmother asked.

"Huh? Uh...sorry. My mind drifted for a second. What'd you say, Gran?"

"I asked if you would deliver the speech for the fundraiser next week. I realize it's short notice, but Dr. Granville broke his leg skiing in Switzerland and won't even be stateside again in time."

"Gran, you know I hate speeches. And hate tuxes even more."

Finn slid into the booth beside his brother. "You and Riley, couple of tux-phobics. What is wrong with the two of you?"

"We're not as uptight as you, hence our more casual formal wear," Brody quipped.

"Nah, you're not as debonair as me." Finn jiggled his tie. "My wife says I make this look sexy."

Brody laughed. "She's biased."

"She is indeed." The same smile that had been on Stace and Riley's faces winged its way across Finn's. Gran sat across from the boys, pleasure lighting her eyes. The whole family was in some kind of happiness time warp. Brody rolled his eyes.

Riley plopped onto the seat beside Gran. "What'd I miss?"

"The hard work." Finn shot him a grin.

"Hey, I've matured. Become a taxpayer, a fiancé *and* a responsible adult, all at the same time."

Brody arched a brow. "You have two of the three. Bummer on the third."

Mary let out an exasperated sigh. "You boys still act like children. My goodness. Celebrate with each other, not tease each other."

Riley pressed a kiss to his grandmother's cheek. "If we did that, we'd have no fun at all, Gran. Besides, Finn and Brody are big boys. They can take whatever I can dish out."

"And deliver it back to you with a second helping," Finn said.

Mary just shook her head, and smiled. "Well as much as I would love to sit here and chat all day with you boys, I do need to get back to the office. So, Brody, will you do the keynote? I think it will do the attendees good to hear about the experiences of someone who actually went overseas and helped people."

Brody swallowed hard. "No one wants to hear what I went through."

His grandmother leaned forward and covered his hand with her own. "You need to talk about it. Maybe if you did—"

"It wouldn't change anything." He shook his head and bit back a curse. "I can't."

His brothers cast him sympathetic looks. "If it helps, we'll sit in the audience and heckle you," Riley joked. "Or just give you a thumbs-up."

Brody shook his head.

"Think about it." Gran got to her feet. Her eyes were kind as she looked down at Brody. "Promise me you'll think about it."

"I will." He intended to do no such thing. But he'd never say that to Gran. He could see the worry in her features, and refused to add to her burdens. He'd find another reason to back out, and line up another speaker for her. That way, she wouldn't be in a bind and he wouldn't be stuck delivering a speech. Maybe Finn would do it for him. "I'll be fine, Gran. And I'll be at the next family dinner."

"Good. And since Riley will be on his honeymoon—"

"Basking on the beach with my beautiful new wife," Riley put in.

"—and we'll have room at the table, I want you to make sure you bring that bakery owner. No excuses."

"Gran, I don't think that's a good idea."

"I want to thank her in person for those chocolates. So don't forget. Sunday afternoon at two. Oh, and when she comes to dinner, tell her to bring more of those chocolates. An old lady needs to have at least one vice, and I've decided mine will be those chocolates." Gran winked, then headed out of the Morning Glory.

Brody tossed some singles on the table for his coffee and started to get to his feet. Finn put a hand on his arm. "I gotta get back to the office."

"You have a minute. I haven't seen you in a while, Brody. And you know, you look like crap."

"Hey!"

"I mean it in the nicest way possible," Finn said.

"He does," Riley added. "Or as nice as Finn can be."

Finn scowled at Riley, then went on. "If you ask me, you've been stewing too much and talking too little. You're a proactive guy, Brody. One who gets in there and makes it right. If you want my advice—"

"I don't." He brushed off Finn's touch. "Thanks for the concern, but I'm doing fine on my own."

"Are you?" Finn asked.

Brody didn't answer. Instead he headed out of the diner. As he did, he realized Finn had a point. Buying a basket of chocolates, bringing cupcakes to a retirement home and adding flour to a mix were not proactive events. None of them were, in fact, in keeping with the kind of thing he normally did. Brody McKenna was a hands-on guy, in a hands-on industry. And until he found something that let him do that, he knew he wouldn't be able to fulfill Andrew's last wishes, or get Kate Spencer moving forward.

And in the process, find a little peace for himself.

CHAPTER SIX

Two days later

HE'D last seen Kate two days ago. And yet, she hadn't been out of his mind once in all that time. He'd come so close to kissing her that night in her shop—too close. He'd called her on Friday, making up an excuse about not being able to help that night, then spent the evening with a bottle of Merlot and a lot of junk TV.

Hadn't changed anything. He still thought about her too much, still worried about her, and still didn't see a way out of the web he'd woven. Finn had been right—he needed a proactive approach to the problem. One that did not involve kissing her.

Brody slipped on a pair of shorts, an old T, and his running shoes, then grabbed his iPod and headed out into the fall sunshine. Most mornings, he had just enough time to run the three mile circuit around his own neighborhood, but on Saturdays, his appointments started later in the morning, which left him extra time to extend his run to the picturesque Chestnut Hill Reservoir.

Dozens of runners, walkers and dog owners strolled the park, greeting the regulars with friendly waves and quick conversations. Late summer flowers peeked through the still green foliage, while the water glistened under the rising sun, twinkling back at him as Brody made the 1.6-mile loop. The sandy packed path was soft under his feet, and soon he slipped into the rhythm of running, oblivious to anyone around him.

He rounded a bend, turning into a gentle breeze skipping over the surface of the water. Ahead of him, Brody spotted a familiar figure.

Kate.

She'd pulled her dark brown hair into a ponytail, and she'd traded her usual jeans and T-shirt for silky navy shorts and a Red Cross T-shirt. Her legs were long and lean, the muscles flexing with each step. She had good form, a steady pace, all signs she ran often. Working off those cupcakes, he presumed. He smiled to himself.

Damn she looked good. Enticing. For the thousandth time, he wished he had kissed her back in the bakery. The magnet of attraction drew him to her again and again. Hunger—yes, that was the word for it—hunger to know her better, to see her more, brewed inside him.

Brody increased his pace until he drew up alongside Kate. "I owe you an apology."

She tugged an earphone out of her ear and glanced over at him. Her skin glistened in the sun. "Brody. I didn't even see you, sorry. I get into a zone when I'm running and don't notice anything around me."

"Me, too." But he had noticed her. He had a feeling no matter what he was doing, he'd be distracted by Kate Spencer. "I wanted to apologize for the other night. You're right. I have no business telling you how to run your life."

She slowed her pace a bit and exhaled. "You might

have been a teensy bit right. I do tend to put in more time at work than I should. And yes, sometimes use work to avoid the hard stuff."

"I can relate to that. Though, sometimes work can be therapeutic."

"True. Or it can be an avoidance technique. Whichever it is, I've got plenty of it to keep me busy." She chuckled. "I appreciate the apology."

He shot her a grin. "You sure you don't want to say anything more? Bash me a bit? Because this is a prime opportunity to get me back by telling me everything I'm doing wrong."

"Oh, I would, but I'm trying to save my breath for running."

He laughed at that. They settled into a comfortable mutual rhythm of running, their steps matching one another as they rounded the sparkling waters of the reservoir. Geese honked as they flew overhead, their bodies forming a perfect V. Brody and Kate neared an empty bench, and slowed their pace.

"I've never seen you running here before," Kate said when they stopped, her words peppered with gasps as she drew in several deep breaths. She propped a leg on one end of the bench and bent forward to stretch.

He did the same on the other end, trying not to watch her. And failing. "During the week, I don't have enough time to make it over here. Most days, I do a quick jog through my neighborhood and then get to work. I run here on the weekends."

"And weekends are my busy time for deliveries, so I get most of my longer runs in during the week." She bent over to stretch her hamstrings, and Brody reminded himself again to be a gentleman and not stare at the creamy length of her legs.

Instead he propped his foot against a nearby post and stretched his calves. Still his gaze stole over to Kate several times, watching as she bent this way and that, working out the lactic acid in her legs.

Beautiful. Absolutely beautiful woman.

And absolutely off limits.

Kate got to her feet, and opened her mouth to say something, then stopped. Her eyes misted, and she turned away. Her body tensed and the good humor left her. Brody's gaze followed where hers had gone.

A dark-haired man in an ARMY T-shirt ran past them, pounding the pavement at a fast clip. He had the crew cut and honed build that spoke of current military service. The close resemblance to Andrew caused a stutter in Brody's chest. Kate paled, and exhaled a long breath.

"Hey," he laid a hand on her shoulder, "you okay?"

"Yeah. That guy over there just looked so much like my brother that for a second I thought..." She shook her head and tried a smile, but it fell flat. "Andrew's gone. Sometimes I forget that. And when I remember..."

"It hurts like hell."

"Yeah." She sighed. "It does."

"Here, sit down for a minute." Brody waved toward the bench, and waited for her to take a seat. In these unguarded moments, Brody got a peek beneath the layers of Kate's grief.

Take care of my sister, Andrew had said. *Don't let her wallow in grief. Make sure she's happy. Living her life.*

"Thank you," she said.

"I'm sorry," Brody said. "I know that's so inade-quate when you're hurting, but I am sorry." The words sat miles away from the true depth of his regret. He watched emotions flicker across her face, and wres-tled with what more to say. A thousand times, he'd had to counsel patients, offer advice. And now, when it counted, he froze.

He knew why. Because he'd started to care about her, had allowed his heart to get tangled.

"Have you ever lost someone you were close to?" Kate asked.

Brody picked a leaf off a low-lying branch near the bench and shredded it as he spoke. "My parents."

"Your parents died? Both of them?"

He nodded. "When I was eight. Car accident. The whole thing was sudden and unexpected." And tough as hell. He hadn't talked about that loss in so long, but there were times, like now, when it hit him all over again.

"You were only eight? Oh, God, that's awful."

"I had my brothers, which made a difference, but yeah, it was still tough." He let out a long breath, and suddenly, he was there again, sandwiched on that overstuffed ugly floral couch in the living room be-tween Finn and Riley while his grandfather delivered the news. Finn, the stoic one, seeming to grow up in an instant, while Riley fidgeted, too young to know better. Brody had stared straight ahead, trying to fit the words into some kind of logical sense, and failing. "I remember when my grandfather told me. It was like my whole world caved in, one wall at a time. Everything I knew was gone, like that." He snapped his fingers. "My grandparents took me and my brothers in. They did their best, but it's never the same as having your mom and dad around, you know?"

"Yeah." She watched the geese settle on the grass across from them, and waddle fat bodies toward the water. "I spent most of my childhood with my grandparents. My parents fought all the time, and Andrew and I hung out in the bakery. To escape, I guess. Then, finally, they got divorced when I was in high school. My dad moved to Florida and my mom moved to Maine, and Andrew and I stayed here with our grandparents. That's part of why Andrew and I were so close. And my grandparents, too. We formed our own little family here."

Andrew had told him that Kate had taken the divorce hard. That she'd been heartbroken at the breakup of the family, as fractured as it was. Andrew had taken it on his shoulders to cheer up his sister, to keep her from dwelling on the major changes in her life. He could see in Kate's face that it still affected her, even after all these years. A childhood interrupted, just like his. "I'm glad you had each other," he said. "Like my brothers and I had each other."

"Yeah. But I don't have him anymore now, do I?" She cursed, let out a long breath, then turned to Brody. "It was my fault, you know." Her eyes filled with tears, and everything in Brody wanted to head off what was coming. "I was the one that encouraged him to sign up. He kept talking about wanting to make a difference, wanting to change lives, and he was such an adventurer, you know? It just seemed perfect. I thought the war was over, how dangerous could it be?" She shook her head and bit her lip. "I shouldn't have said anything. I should have—"

She cursed. Brody ached to tell her the truth, but how could he do that without adding to her pain? Recount the story of Andrew's death, and his part in that moment, and see her go through that loss all over again. He bit his tongue and listened instead.

"A part of me feels like…" at this her eyes misted again, and Brody wanted to both hold her and run for the hills, "if I hadn't encouraged him, if I had told him to become a hiking instructor or skydiver or something instead, he'd be here today."

He put a hand on her shoulder. "Kate. It's not your fault. Your brother loved—"

"My brother died because of me, don't you see that?" Tears streamed down her cheeks, and she swiped them away with a quick, hard movement. "I'm the one that encouraged him, pushed him. If I never said a word, he'd be here today and I'd…"

He reached for her hand. "You'd what?"

She exhaled, a long, slow breath. "I'd forgive myself."

Brody's heart ached for her. How he knew that pain. That guilt. "You can't blame yourself, Kate. People do what they want to do. Andrew was an adult. If he didn't want to join, he would have told you. You said yourself he loved his job."

She shook her head. "Every day, I live with that regret. Every day, I wish I could take the words back. I go to work and I stand there, and I wish I could do it over. It's like I'm standing in cement, and no matter how hard I try, I can't pick my feet up again." Pain etched Kate's features. Brody saw now why Andrew had been so adamant about protecting his sister. She did blame herself, and the worst thing Brody could do was add to that burden.

I don't want her blaming herself or dwelling on the past. I want her eyes on the future. Encourage her to take a risk, to pursue her dreams. Don't let her spend one more second grieving or regretting.

Andrew's words came back to him. Somehow, Brody needed to find a way to redirect Kate's emotional rudder.

She sat for a moment, then shifted in her seat to face him. "Before the soldiers even knocked on my door, I knew. I fell apart right then, a sobbing messy puddle on the floor. That pain," she exhaled a long, shaky breath, "that pain was excruciating. As if someone had ripped out my heart right in front of me." She drew her knees up to her chest, and hugged her arms around her shins. "What if I'd said 'be careful' one more time, or told him I loved him again? Would it have ended differently?"

"I think you did everything you could. Sometimes… these things just happen." Every instinct in him wanted to make this better for her, to ease her pain. And somehow do it without violating the promise he had made. "When I was in med school, I lost a patient. I'd seen him a couple times before, and had gotten to know him during the time I was working there."

It was a story Brody had never fully told before. The words halted in his throat, but he pushed them forward. He had promised to help Kate, and maybe, just maybe, knowing she wasn't alone would do that. "He loved to walk the city," Brody went on. "But he was legally blind, and in a city that busy…"

"Accidents happened."

Brody nodded. "Construction projects springing up

out of nowhere create obstacles that he couldn't see or anticipate. He had a cane, and was thinking about getting a guide dog, when he was hit by a car."

"Oh, Brody. That's awful."

"He was just crossing the street. One of those senseless deaths that shouldn't happen." Brody sighed and shook his head. "I tried so hard to keep that man alive. So damned hard. I kept pushing on his chest, up, down, up, down, yelling at him to hold, to keep trying, don't die on me—"

At some point he'd stopped talking about the patient in Boston. His mind had gone back to that dusty hut in Afghanistan, to a moment that could have been a carbon copy of the one at Mass General. Young man, cut down in the prime of his life, and Brody, powerless to prevent his death.

"It was too late," Brody went on, his voice low, hoarse. In that instant, he didn't see the pedestrian hit by a car, he saw Andrew's eyes again. So like Kate's. Wide, trusting, believing the doctor tending to his wounds would know what to do. So sure that Brody could save his life. "It's in your hands, doc," Andrew had said. He'd given Brody his life—

And Brody had let him down.

Brody heard the choppers in his head, the pounding of the rotors, the shouting of the other soldiers. Heard himself calling out to the other doctors, asking for supplies they didn't have. Too many wounded at one time, too few resources, and too few miracles available. Brody flexed his palms, but he could still feel Andrew's chest beneath his hands. The furious pumping to try to bring him back, and the silent, still response.

"They had to stop me from doing CPR," Brody said.

The other doctor, pulling him off, telling him it was too late. There was no hope. "I just...I wanted him to live so bad, but it wasn't enough. Not enough at all."

Now her hand covered his, sympathetic, understanding. "Oh, Brody, I'm so sorry."

On the other side of the reservoir, Brody saw the gray flash of the soldier's T-shirt moving down the path. Guilt and regret settled hard and bitter in Brody's stomach. Did he want to see Kate living with that the rest of her life?

He wasn't here to assuage his own pain. He was here to help her with hers.

"How did you..." she took a breath, let it out again, "how did you get past that loss?"

"For a long time, I blamed myself," Brody said, his mind drifting back to those difficult days in med school. "For a while, I thought I should do something else, something outside of medicine. I felt so damned guilty, like you do."

She nodded, mute.

"He was always joking, that patient of mine. It got so that I even kidded him about walking the streets of Boston, told him to keep an eye out. He thought that was the funniest damned thing he ever heard. It became a running joke between us. He'd thank me for stitching him up and joke that he'd be back for another appointment next week. I did the same thing you did, Kate, I blamed myself. What if I didn't joke with him? What if I'd lectured him about being careful?" He tossed the remains of the leaf onto the ground and turned to her. "For weeks, I was stuck, like you. Then I realized I wasn't doing myself, or his memory, any good." His gaze swept over Kate's delicate features. He thought of all she had told him in the last few days, and of what Finn had said. Do something proactive. That was what Brody had done all those years ago, and what Kate needed to do now. "I ended up going down to city hall and petitioning them for an audio crosswalk at the intersection where my patient was hit. The kind that beeps, warns people with vision problems. It might have been too late for him, but it wasn't for the next person. Doing that helped me a lot. It made me move forward."

"That's what I need to do." She sighed. "Someday."

Then he knew how he could help her. How he could get her out of that self-imposed cement. Something bigger, better than baking cupcakes and delivering desserts. "How do you feel about taking a trip to Weymouth this afternoon?"

"Weymouth? Why?"

"Let's go look at that location you were considering. See if it's good enough for another Nora's Sweet Shop."

"Oh, Brody, I can't—"

"Can't? Or won't? I'll be done with patients at three, and last I checked, the sign on the door said you close at three. I'd say that's a sign we should go. Do something proactive, Kate, and maybe..." his hand covered hers, "maybe then you can move forward again."

She studied him for a second then a smile curved across her face. "You're not going to let me say no, are you?"

"Not on your life."

"Okay. Meet me at the shop at three. I'll give the realtor a call this morning."

He got to his feet, put out a hand and hauled her to her feet, too. Now she stood close, so close, a strong breeze would have brought them together. His thoughts swirled around the sweet temptation of Kate Spencer. Her emerald eyes, her beautiful smile, her slender frame. And then to her lips, parted slightly, as if begging him to kiss them. How he wanted to, and oh how he shouldn't. "Then it's a date."

A date.

Kate pondered those words all day while she worked. Joanne had called and said she'd be tied up for a few more days with her daughter. "She's finding out a new baby is a lot more exhausting than she thought," Joanne said, "and my son-in-law couldn't take any more time off from work to help her. Are you sure you're going to be okay without me?"

"I have temporary help," Kate said. "You just enjoy that new grandbaby." She and Joanne chatted a bit more about the new baby, then Kate hung up. She glanced at the clock, saw the hands slowly marking time until Brody arrived.

Nerves fluttered in her stomach. Crazy. He might have used the word *date,* but that didn't mean he meant it. They were going to look at a piece of real estate, for goodness' sake, not go dancing.

That word conjured up the memory of dancing with Brody, of being in his strong, capable arms, pressed to his broad, muscled chest. He'd had a sure step, a confident swing, and when she'd been in his arms, she'd felt—

Safe. Treasured.

Nope, nope, nope. Her goal today involved real estate, not potential husbands.

Still, a part of her really liked Brody. He'd told her not all doctors were the same, and the more she got to know him, the more she wondered if he was that one rare animal in the room. Could this man who volunteered in needy areas, who'd taken the time to help a stressed out baker, could he be the one for her? Or too good to be true?

The last thing she wanted to do was repeat her mother's mistakes and rush into a relationship that was doomed from the start, then spend the rest of her life fighting to make it into something it could never be. Better to be cautious, to find a quiet, gentle man. Not one who sent her heart into overdrive.

Easier said than done.

Kate fussed with her hair. Checked her lipstick twice. Rethought her choice of a skirt instead of jeans at least a dozen times. Ever since she'd met Brody, her mind had been working against her resolve to business only. First peppering her dreams with images of him, then flashing to his smile, his eyes, at the oddest times. She was hooked, and hooked but good.

A little after one, the bell over the door rang, and Kate had to force herself not to break out in a huge smile when Brody walked into the shop. "You're here early. I thought you said you wouldn't be over until three."

"My one o'clock appointment canceled, and I had an hour until the next one, so I thought I'd stop by and see how you were doing."

Thoughtful. Sweet. Because he liked her? "It's been a busy day."

"Too busy for lunch?" He held up a bag from a local sub shop.

She snatched it out of his hands. "Bless you. I was about to eat the fixtures." She glanced up at him, trying to read the intent behind his blue eyes. "You're always taking care of me."

"I'm trying to, Kate." His gaze met hers and held.

"Well, thank you." The intensity in his eyes rocked her, and she turned on her heel, heading for the kitchen, rather than deal with the simmering tension between them.

He followed her out back and sat across from her while she ate.

She finished up the sandwich. "Thank you again. I don't think I've ever eaten that fast in my life. And one more healthy meal from Doctor McKenna. This is becoming a habit."

"All part of the service, ma'am." He grinned. "Besides, it'll be on my bill."

She laughed. "Well maybe I should charge you for cupcakes consumed."

"Who me?" He snatched one of the miniature ones she'd just frosted, and popped it in his mouth. "I don't know what you're talking about. Show me the evidence."

"I'll do better than that." She wagged a finger at him. "I'll make you work harder next time we're in this kitchen."

He glanced around the room, at the stacks of orders on the counter, the tubs of supplies waiting by the mixer. "If you want, we can tackle whatever is on your To Do list after we see that property today."

"That would make for a really long day. Wouldn't that interfere with your plans?"

"Plans?"

A flush filled her cheeks. She got to her feet, and tossed her trash into the bin. "Well, it's Saturday and

I didn't want to assume you didn't have…" *Push the words out, Kate, you'll never know unless you ask,* "a date or anything."

"I don't have a date." He came over to her, lowered the apron to the counter. "Not tonight."

"What about tomorrow night?" Who was this forward woman? Hadn't she vowed a thousand times not to get involved with a man like him? To be cautious, look for someone who didn't inspire her to run off to the nearest bedroom? But a part of her wondered if Brody was different, if the risk in falling for him would end in the kind of love story her grandparents had enjoyed. And that part wanted to get that answer. Very, very badly.

"Not tomorrow night, either. I'm not dating anyone right now." He reached up a hand and captured the end of her ponytail, letting it slide through his fingers. She inhaled the dark woodsy scent of his cologne. "In fact, I don't even have a date for my own brother's wedding."

"That's too bad. Especially if there's dancing." A smile curved across her face. "I bet Tabitha is free."

"I'd much rather take someone closer to my own age. Someone who could use a night off." He twirled the end of her hair around his finger, his blue eyes locked on hers. "Someone like you."

Her heart hammered in her chest. Her pulse tripped. She reminded herself—twice—to breathe. "Are you asking me on a real date, Brody McKenna?"

"I am indeed."

Now the smile she'd been trying to hold back did wing its way across her face. Her heart sputtered, then soared. "Then I accept."

"Good." His hands took hers, and he pulled her to

him. "You know, I haven't been able to stop thinking about you all day. I would be talking to a patient, and end up thinking about you. Or I'd be trying to write up my notes, and think about you. I even called poor Mrs. Maguire Kate today instead of Helen."

"Because of my cupcakes?"

He traced a finger along her face, down her jaw, over her lips. She breathed, and when her lips parted, his finger lingered on her lower lip. Tempting. "Because of your smile. Because of your eyes. Because of the way you make me hope and dream of things I…well, I hadn't wanted before. You…you're not what I expected."

Another odd comment. Brody McKenna seemed full of them. The man had more dimensions than a layer cake. "What you expected?" She laughed. "It seems my reputation has preceded me, if you had expectations." She lifted her jaw to his, sassy, teasing. "Have other people been talking about me and saying I'm this boring old fuddy duddy who does nothing but work?"

"That's not it."

"Then what expectations did you have? Because you seem to have a heck of a bead on everything about me. As if you knew me before you met me."

The humor dropped from his face, and he took a step back, releasing her hands. He turned away, facing the wall where she had hung the plaques and reviews of the shop. "I'm not…not who you think I am, Kate."

"Not a doctor?" She grinned. "Don't tell me you're actually a nurse."

"No, no, it's not that. It's—"

A ding sounded from the oven. "Oh, the cupcakes are done. I have to get them out of the oven or they'll burn." Kate pivoted to take the trays of baked cupcakes out of the oven and set them on the racks to cool. "God, what a busy day. Good thing you're taking me to Weymouth this afternoon, or I'd be liable to work until I passed out. In case you haven't noticed, I'm still working on the prioritizing thing. Like learning to add a little fun into my day and keep my eye on the bigger goal."

"Which is?"

She placed her hands on the counter and glanced out the window at the clear blue sky. "Continue the legacy my grandparents started, while learning not to waste a second of my life on grief. Someone gave me some advice about that today, and I'm still trying to take it in." She gave Brody a watery smile. "I'm working on it anyway."

"Good." Brody handed her another batch ready to go, then helped her load liners and batter into the next set of cupcake pans.

"So, what'd you want to tell me?" she asked. "What did you mean when you said you're not who I think you are?"

He gave her that grin she was beginning to know as well as her own. "Well, first, that I'm not a baker, not by any stretch."

"That I noticed." She sensed shadows lurking behind Brody's words, like secret passages that led to parts of himself he'd closed off. She wanted to quiz him, wanted to press him, but the cupcakes were waiting to be frosted, and the orders were piled up, and time was of the essence if she hoped to get out of here on time. So Kate let it drop for now, intending to come back to serious topics when they had more time.

Kate added a pink fondant flower to the top of one of the baked treats. "I used to send care packages to

Andrew's unit overseas, and one time, I sent him a whole batch of cookies with pink flowers on top, as a joke. He said they were the best damned thing he and the guys ever ate, and asked me to send more. So I did. Pink and blue and purple flowers. He said it was like a garden exploded when he opened the box." She laughed, then shook her head, as the laugh turned to tears. "Oh, damn. See what I mean? I'm trying, but I'm not doing so good at the last one. I miss him. God, do I miss him."

Brody turned to her at the same time she turned to him. He gathered her to his chest, and she let the tears fall. She'd promised herself she'd never again rely on a man, never fall fast and hard, but Brody seemed different. Like the kind of man she could trust. Lean into. Depend upon.

Then like a wave, the loss of her brother hit her all over again. He was gone, and she'd never again see his smile or hear him tease her, or look for treasures in the yard. He was gone…and she was here, without him.

"Andrew was the strong one, you know? When our parents got divorced, he was the one who told me it'd all be okay. He was the one who dragged me down to the bakery day after day. He saved me." She shook her head, tears smearing into the cotton of his shirt. "I don't know what I would have done without him. And I don't know what I'll do without him now."

"You'll go on, and put one foot in front of the other. Because he would want that."

She raised her gaze to Brody's. Damn. This man read her like a book. "He would."

"He'd want you to keep running this shop and keep your family's legacy going. He'd want you to go look at that location this afternoon, and move toward the future. He wouldn't want you to stand around and cry for him."

"You talk like you know him." She swiped at her face. "That's exactly what Andrew would say. Actually, he'd say it far more direct and with far more colorful language." She laughed, and the sorrow that had gripped her began to ease a bit. "I wish you had met him. He was an amazing man."

"I feel like I have met him," Brody said quietly. "He's in every part of this shop and everything you do and… it's like he's here with us."

"It is." She bit her lip and nodded. "Thank you for lunch, for being here, for cheering me up."

"Kate—" The clock on the wall chimed quarter to the hour, at the same time Brody's cell phone began to vibrate. "Damn. My time's up. I have to get back to the office for the last couple of appointments." He pressed a kiss to her lips, then cupped her jaw. "I'll be back. And we'll talk then, okay?"

"I can't wait." And as she watched Brody McKenna leave, Kate thought there was nothing closer to the truth than that.

She was beginning to fall for the doctor, and fall hard.

CHAPTER SEVEN

ONE hour later, true to his word, Brody returned to the shop. The sight of him caused a hitch in Kate's breath. "You're on time," she said. "Quite impressive for a doctor."

He chuckled. "That's a pet peeve of mine. I hate to be late, for anything, and I work hard to make sure my practice runs on time. Makes for happier patients—"

"And a happier doctor."

"That, too." He swung his car keys around his finger. "You ready? I thought I'd drive, so you could concentrate on the building and neighborhood."

Thoughtful. Nice. Again. Did the man like her, or just see a pity case?

And why did she keep wondering about that?

"I won't turn that offer down." She tucked her apron behind the counter then headed out of the shop behind him, locking the door as she left. At the curb, Brody opened the passenger side door of an older Jeep, its dark green paint a little worse for wear. "What, no Mercedes?"

"I told you. I'm not the typical doctor. This is the car that got me through my college years, and I've had it so long, it's part of the family." He shrugged. "Whether

I can afford a Mercedes or not isn't the point. I don't need a sixty thousand dollar piece of metal to prove I'm successful. I'd rather let my patients speak to that."

"You are different," she said. "In a good way." She got into the Jeep, and waited while Brody came around to the driver's side. Every time Kate thought she had him pigeonholed, he added another dimension to his character. Maybe she'd misjudged him. Seen him through jaded eyes. Every minute she spent with him, Brody McKenna came closer to the kind of man she thought didn't exist.

Still, she suspected Brody McKenna kept a part of himself back. She wasn't sure what it was, or why he was keeping himself distanced from her, but she knew better than to try to force a bridge when there was only a rope across the river between them. If he was interested, he'd open up, and if he didn't...

She didn't need to fall for a mystery. Her mother had made that mistake, and she refused to do the same.

"So, tell me about this property." Brody put the Jeep in gear—a stick shift, which impressed Kate a little more—and pulled away from the curb.

"It's a thousand square feet, which is pretty much the same size I have now, and it's on a corner lot, beside a coffee shop and a florist. Busy location, with a lot of foot traffic."

"Sounds perfect. And like the kind of location that would let you do some partnering and cross-marketing with your neighbors." He flashed her a grin. "Sometimes I listened when my grandparents talked about work."

Kate laughed. "We'll see. I've looked at it online, and talked to the realtor a few weeks back, but this is my first in-person visit. Sometimes what you get in person isn't as good as the advertisement."

"Sort of like online dating, huh?"

"Speaking from personal experience, Doctor?" Curiosity about Brody's dating past sparked inside her. What had kept such an eligible, smart, handsome man from marrying? Was he really that gun-shy or had he been burned before, like her?

"Nope, can't say I've ever tried that," he said. "I'm old-fashioned. I like to meet people, see if there's a connection, and then take the next step."

"You said you came close to settling down before. What happened to that connection?"

Brody sighed. "Melissa and I got engaged right out of college, then I went on my first medical mission trip, and she broke up with me while I was gone."

"She did? Why?"

"She expected that being a doctor's wife meant shopping on Fifth Avenue and vacationing in Italy, not visiting third world countries to treat malaria and set broken bones. And, I was distant, and didn't put in the time I should have with the relationship." He sighed. "I tried to fix things, but I was too late."

"And that burned you forever on the idea of love?"

"That and…a few other things. I guess at a certain point, I gave up on finding someone who shared my goals."

She chuckled. "Now you sound like me. Two jaded souls. Destined for…"

"What?" he asked.

"I don't know. You tell me."

He raised and lowered a shoulder, a grin playing on

his lips. "Last I checked, psychic abilities weren't on my résumé."

She laughed. "No fair. You can't go all mysterious on me."

"Me? Mysterious? I'm as easy to read as a prescription."

That made her laugh even harder. "Written in a doctor's handwriting? That makes it illegible."

"I never said figuring me out would be easy." He grinned.

"Oh, I agree. You are far from easy to decipher. You're a Sphinx with a stethoscope." Kate sat back against the seat, wondering about this other side of her that being around Brody encouraged. She didn't trade flirty repartee with men. She worked hard, kept her nose to the grindstone, and yes came up for air once in a while to go on a date. But never had she met a man who made her exchange...

Banter.

Or met a man who made her blush like a schoolgirl. A man who made butterflies flutter in her stomach. A man who made her begin to dream again of things she'd given up on long ago. Not like this, she hadn't. A part of her threw up a huge Caution side while another part craved more.

The whole ride to Weymouth went like that, the two of them exchanging barbs, always with a hint of flirting on the side. The sun shone bright, and Brody had the windows down, letting in a nice fresh breeze. When they turned off on the Route 18 exit, disappointment filled Kate as they neared their destination.

A few minutes later—and after getting turned around once—they pulled in front of the location, a cute little storefront smack dab in a part of Weymouth dubbed Columbian Square. From the historic homes bordering the square to the old style storefronts, Kate could see vestiges of Weymouth's historic roots. Across the street from the shop sat the Cameo Theater, an old-style movie house that harkened back to the days of Model T cars. "Quaint, isn't it?"

"It looks perfect for a second Nora's." Brody came around and opened her door then the two of them headed for the storefront. People walked along the sidewalk, popping in and out of shops, chatting and enjoying the warm fall day. Traffic slowed at the stop signs, drivers casting quick glances at the shop wares before continuing on their way.

A wiry dark-haired man came hustling down the street, a packet of papers under one arm, a briefcase in the opposite hand. He extended his free hand as he came upon Kate and Brody. "Hello, hello. You must be Miss…Spencer? Here about the building?"

"Kate Spencer." She shook with the other man. "Owner of Nora's Sweet Shop in Newton. Thank you for meeting me today."

"No problem." He turned to Brody and shook. "I'm Bill Taylor." He turned and unlocked the door, then led them inside. "Nora's Sweet Shop, you said? Sounds like just the thing for our little community. We have lots of shops here that can compliment a bakery. And with the hospital around the corner, there's always a demand for gift baskets and the like."

As Bill talked about square footage and lighting, Kate took the time to look around, to imagine a counter here, a display there. The shop had housed a deli before, and the kitchen would need minimal changes to meet Kate's needs. All in all, the shop had the space and equipment to house another Nora's, not to mention a prime location.

"Looks perfect," Brody said to Kate. "Not that I'm an expert in these kinds of things, but it sure seems ideal to me."

"It is perfect. Right town, right space, right location."

"And right for you now?" Bill asked, already reaching into his stash of papers for an offer sheet.

Kate looked around. Nerves threatened to choke her. Brody had told her to be proactive, but now that the moment to take that step forward had arrived, she stalled. "I, um, I don't know. I need some time to think about it." She thanked Bill for his time, promised to call the realtor with any other questions, then headed out to the car. Brody opened her door, then climbed in the driver's seat.

"Why didn't you make an offer?" he asked. "I thought you said that place was perfect."

"I just don't think now is the right time to be adding locations." She watched the storefront grow smaller as the Jeep headed down the street. A mixture of disappointment and relief washed over her. Disappointment that she'd let the location go. Relief that she didn't have to tackle a major task like a second location. Maybe next month. Or the month after. Maybe she'd wait till spring when the weather improved, and people spent more time strolling the streets. Valid reasons? Or stall tactics?

"Do you want to talk about it?" Brody asked.

No, she didn't, but Brody had driven her here and deserved an answer. Maybe if she got her reservations out on the table, the worries would ease.

"It's scary to take that next step, you know?" she

said. "And I'm just not sure that I'm ready for it. I mean, adding a second location splits me in two, and I have my hands full with the Newton location as it is."

"Your assistant will be back soon, and you talked about hiring others, so that will free up your time," he pointed out. "I agree that the next step is scary as hell. You could fail, or you could succeed. But you won't know either unless you try."

She watched the streets of Weymouth pass by outside the window. Neat houses in neat rows, flanked by businesses on either side. A bustling, growing community, one that seemed much like Newton. One that could support a Nora's Sweet Shop, if she dared to make the attempt.

Fail...or succeed. Either prospect sent a shiver of worry down her spine. She turned to Brody. "How did you do it?"

Brody flipped on the directional, then merged onto the interstate. His gaze remained on the road, his hand shifting the gear as they accelerated and entered the fray of automobiles. "Do what?"

"Take those risks, fly to other cities, other countries, and step into a strange environment? How did you know it would work out?"

"I didn't. I had to trust in my skills as a doctor. And sometimes, I succeeded. And sometimes," he let out a long, low breath, "I failed."

"That's what I'm most afraid of, I guess. Andrew was the risk taker, the one who would go all in on everything from poker to tic-tac-toe." She fiddled with the strap on her purse. Andrew had traveled the world, leapt out of airplanes, climbed mountains. While all her life, Kate had stayed in the same town, worked in the same business, seen the same people, baked the same things. "I know he'd want me to do it, but…"

"You're afraid of letting him down."

"Yeah." She sighed. "And myself. And my grandmother. And all those people who love Nora's Sweet Shop."

"I can relate to that. When someone gives you a huge responsibility, it can be scary. You worry about whether you are up to the task. Whether you'll fulfill their wishes, the way they wanted. Whether…you're doing the right thing at all." Little traffic filled the highway, few people traveling in or out of the city on a fall Saturday afternoon. "Maybe you should wait then. Give it a little time."

"Maybe." Or maybe she should throw caution to the wind, as Andrew had done, and just go for it. Leap off the edge and trust the winds to carry her.

As the miles clicked by and the city drew closer, Kate realized she didn't want the day to end. Brody had been good company, and joking with him on the way out here had brightened her day, eased the tension in her shoulders. Whenever she spent time with him, he had the same effect. He made her forget, made her think about the day ahead, rather than the past.

She liked him, as a friend, and as something more, something she wanted to explore, taste. She wondered about the things he kept to himself, wondered how it fit with the man she'd gotten to know. "I'm not sure what your plan is for today, but if you're free, I'd like to invite you over for dinner. Nothing too fancy, because I'm not exactly cook of the year, but it'll be edible, I promise."

"I've tasted your cupcakes. You can definitely cook."

"Bake, not cook. They're two different sciences. I'm

great with things that are exact and precise, but with cooking, a lot of it is a pinch of this, a dash of that, and it gets me all flustered." She shook her head. "Don't even ask me about the Thanksgiving turkey debacle."

He laughed. "Now that I'd like to see. You flustered."

"You'll see that, and the parts of my life that aren't so organized." Inviting him over meant opening a door to herself. She hadn't done that in a long, long time. She thought of her brother, and how he approached his days with a what's-the-worst-that-could-happen attitude, and decided she'd take a cue from Andrew, and dance a little closer to the edge of danger.

"You'll be shattering my image of you as the perfect woman, you know," Brody said.

She pivoted in her seat. "You think I'm the perfect woman?"

He turned toward her, but his eyes remained unreadable behind dark sunglasses. "I think you're pretty damned amazing."

Her face heated, and a smile winged across her face. Her heart skipped, as if she'd been rocketed back to middle school and the cute boy in math class had dropped a note on her desk. "Amazing, huh? You're not so bad yourself, Doctor."

"Well, there's a rousing endorsement." He laughed. "I'll have to add that to my online dating profile."

She gave him a coy smile. "I can't be throwing out compliments left and right at you. You could get a swelled head."

"I doubt that's going to happen. I have my brothers to remind me that I can still be a dork sometimes."

"You? A dork? I don't think so." She took in the sharp line of his jaw, his tousled dark hair, his defined, strong hands. The last word she'd use to describe Brody was *dork*. Sexy, mysterious, intriguing, tempting...

A hundred other words came to mind when she looked at Brody McKenna.

"Hey, don't underestimate me. I read medical journals in my spare time. And watch operation shows on TV. I've never been in the cool kids clique." He grinned.

She waved that off. "That's overrated if you ask me."

He grinned. "Oh, were you in the cool kids group?"

"I was a cheerleader." She shrugged. "Membership came with the pom-poms."

"You were a cheerleader?" A grin quirked up on one side of his face. "You do know that when you tell a man that, it gives him ideas?"

"Does it help to know I was terrible at it?"

He thought a second. "Ummm...nope."

"Well, just don't ask me to rah-rah and we'll get along just fine."

"Even if I say please?"

"Even if you say please." She laughed, but still a simmering sexual tension filled the car, rife with the innuendos and unspoken desires hanging between them. Maybe later, she'd explore a little of that with Brody McKenna. Take a chance for once, and let the man not just into her house, but into her heart.

They neared her exit, and she gave Brody directions. In a few minutes, he had reached the driveway of her townhome. "Home sweet home," he said, and shut off the engine. The Jeep clicked a few times, then fell silent.

Nerves bubbled inside her. She'd invited men into her home before, but this time seemed different. Because she'd started to like Brody—a lot? Because being around an enticing man like Brody embodied taking a risk?

Either way, the few steps it took to get from the driveway to the front door seemed to last forever. She unlocked the door, then flicked on the hall light and stepped inside, with Brody following. "Can I get you something to drink?"

"Sure."

"Um, beer, water, soda?"

He opted for water. She filled two glasses, then led him to the small sunroom at the back of her townhouse. Screened in the summer, shuttered in the winter, the room offered large windows and a fabulous peek of the outdoors. "This is my favorite room. It's not very big, but it has a fabulous view." She waved toward the picture windows, and the thick copse of woods that ran along the back of the property. She'd hung birdfeeders on several of the trees when she first moved in, which provided a constant flurry of winged activity.

Brody sat on an overstuffed floral patterned love-seat, a tall man on a feminine couch. Somehow, Brody made it work. "I can see why you love it," he said. "It's hard to get something like this so close to the city, with woods and everything. Sitting here must be a nice way for you to unwind."

"It is. I've spent many an afternoon or evening out here, reading a book or just listening to music and watching the birds. It's…"

"Calming," Brody said.

"Yes. Very." Except with Brody in the room, calm didn't describe the riot of awareness rocketing through her. Her mind went back to that almost kiss the other day. For the hundredth time, she wished they'd finished what they'd started.

Who was Brody McKenna? Between the flirting and the compliments and the help in the bakery, he seemed interested in her, but when it came to moving things to the next level, he backed away instead. Was she misreading him?

"When I was in…" he stopped, started again, "overseas, we stopped in this tiny village for several days. It sat in this little oasis, a valley of sorts, nestled between several mountain ranges." As he spoke, she had the feeling in his mind, he'd gone to that destination, and his voice softened with the memory. "Not many places over there had trees, but this one did. The room where I stayed looked out over a stone wall and a field, all shadowed by the majesty of the mountains. When the sun rose, it painted an exquisite picture. Gold washing over purple, then over green, like unrolling a blanket of yellow. It was simple and beautiful."

"It sounds it."

"The days there were long, and tough." He ran a hand through his hair and sighed. "Some days, that mountain range restored my sanity, brought me back to reality. To what mattered."

"My brother talked about something similar. He said that every day he spent in Afghanistan, he made it a point to find something beautiful wherever he went. And when things got tough, he'd just focus on that one beautiful thing, and it would remind him of home and why he was there."

"Those moments brought him peace?"

"I think they did." She looked at Brody McKenna and saw a man who needed that same kind of peace.

He carried a load of troubles on his shoulders. What troubles, she wasn't sure, but she suspected it stemmed from a recent tragic event. Maybe she could help him find a little solace, or if nothing else, show him she understood. He was trying to do that for her, and the least she could do was the same.

Kate got to her feet, and crossed to a cedar box that sat on the shelf. All this time, the box had sat, closed, waiting for her to be ready. To open it, to share the contents, to tell the story. She realized as she carried the small wooden container back to the loveseat, that for a month, she'd put her emotions on a back burner. She'd done that long enough.

"I want to show you something." Kate settled herself beside Brody, and opened the lid. "I haven't shown this to anyone, except my grandmother." She pulled out a trio of velvet boxes, and laid them on the coffee table. "Andrew's medals, given posthumously. Odd word, isn't that? Posthumously. Like it was funny afterwards or something." She shook her head, then reached into the box, and withdrew another item. "The flag from his funeral." She placed the triangular folded item on the table, giving it one lingering touch then reached inside one more time. "And the four leaf clover necklace he wore. He called it his good luck charm."

Brody remembered.

In that moment, he was back in the first village they'd stayed in, sitting outside, watching the sun go down behind the mountains. Andrew sat beside him, fingering the necklace. The clover had caught the last of the sun's rays, bouncing them off like an aura. Brody had asked Andrew about the emblem, and that conversation had built the beginnings of a friendship between the two men.

The memory sent a rush of emotion through Brody. He glanced at the necklace in Kate's hand. The explosion had chipped off one corner, twisted another, doing the same damage to the jewelry as it had done inside Andrew's body. He could see Andrew all over again, lying on the ground, torn apart by the blast, while his friends lay nearby. Blood mingled with fear, and Brody and the other doctor with him rushing to try and save them all. Knowing at least one would die before the day ended.

Brody's throat grew thick, his eyes burned. "You okay?" Kate asked, placing a hand on his arm. Her comforting him, when he should be the one comforting her.

"Yeah." A lie. He hadn't been okay in a long time, and the necklace brought back all the reasons why. "My father used to have a four leaf clover necktie. He wore it whenever he called on a new client." Brody had shared the same story with Andrew, all those weeks ago and sharing it now with Kate was like being back there on that porch while the sun sent the world a goodnight kiss. "One of us inherited the tie when my father died. Finn, I think. We're Irish, so you know the four-leaf clover superstition is alive and well."

"Andrew just liked them. When we were kids, we spent an entire afternoon, combing the yard, looking for one." She ran her thumb over the four heart shapes that converged to form the trademark leaves. "We never found one, but we tried our best."

"Maybe that's because luck isn't something you find. It's something you…create."

"True." She gave the necklace one last touch then

lowered it to the table, one link at a time. "That's why I don't want to open another location. Because I'm afraid that..."

When she didn't go on, he turned to her, took one of her hands in his and waited until her gaze met his. "Afraid of what?"

"Afraid that I'll be as unlucky as Andrew." The truth sat there, cold, stark. "That I'll take a risk and I'll fail, and I'll..." Her hand ran over the folded surface of the flag, "Let him down. Let myself down."

"You're smart, Kate. Talented as hell. And you have something that people love and enjoy. That's a recipe for success." He closed her palm over the charm. "With or without a good luck charm, you're going to do just fine."

"I hope you're right." She gave him a watery smile. "There are days when it's hard to find that view, and focus on the good."

"I know what you mean. I don't think I've seen that view in a long, long time."

She gave the box a loving touch then raised her gaze to Brody's. "I shared all this with you because I wanted you to know that I understand what it's like to need that one little thing that restores your sanity, gets you back on track. I don't know what's bothering you, but it's clear something is weighing heavy on your shoulders." She picked up the necklace and dropped it into Brody's palm. "I want you to have this. Let it be your view, Brody. It worked for Andrew, and I'm sure it'll work for you."

The gold weighed heavy in his palm. "I...I can't take this, Kate."

"But—"

Brody glanced at the medals, the flag, lying on the

table, and knew he could delay this no longer. Kate deserved to know the truth, even if it hurt. Even if it went against her brother's wishes. Maybe Andrew was wrong. Maybe his sister could handle more than he'd thought.

"Kate, there's something I want to tell you." Against Brody's hip, his cell phone began to ring, the distinctive trilling tone that meant his service was trying to reach him. Routine calls, like appointment changes, were routed to voicemail, but emergencies went straight to Brody's cell. He cursed under his breath. "I have to get this."

He flipped out the phone, and answered it. In seconds, the operator relayed the information—one of his patients had landed in the hospital a few minutes ago with heart attack symptoms. The cardiac team wanted the primary care physician's input before proceeding. "I'll be right there." He closed the phone and put it back in the holster. "I'm sorry. I have to go."

"Duty calls?"

He nodded. "It's an emergency. Listen, I'll catch up with you tomorrow, okay?"

"I can't. My grandparents and I are going up to Maine for the day to visit my mom. How about Monday?"

"I'll be there." Even though he dreaded the conversation he needed to have with her, a part of him couldn't wait to see her again. Today had been fun, and brought an unexpected lightness to his heart. He craved more of that.

Craved more of Kate.

"You'll be there on Monday, with your apron on?" She gave him a teasing wink.

He chuckled. "Of course. I'm starting to see it as the

next best fashion accessory. What all the cool docs will be wearing this winter."

She led him to the door, then paused and put a hand on his arm. Her gentle touch warmed his skin. "Brody?"

"Yeah?"

"Thank you for today. You made me laugh, and you made me forget, and it was...wonderful." A smile curved across her face, this one a sweet, easy smile. "I needed that. A lot."

All Andrew Spencer had wanted was his older sister's happiness. Brody had done his best to ensure that, and to ensure she followed the path she'd been on before she lost her brother. A win in that column, but a loss in the other, where the truth lay. And complicating the equation—

Brody liked Kate Spencer. A lot. He wanted more, wanted to make her his. Wanted to take her in his arms and kiss her until neither of them could see straight. To do that, he had to start them off on the right foot—

And tell her why he had walked into her shop that first day. Was she ready to hear the truth? Or would it set her back even more?

His phone buzzed a second time, reminding him the patient came first. Before what Brody wanted, before what Brody craved. And that meant any relationship with Kate Spencer fell far down the line from the promise Brody had made in that dusty hut.

CHAPTER EIGHT

THE Morning Glory Diner promised good home cooked meals according to the sign in the window and the delicious scents emanating every time someone opened the door. Kate stepped inside, and opted for a table by the window. The flowers of the namesake ringed the bright diner's walls and decorated everything from the menus to the napkin holders. The counters were a soft pale yellow, the seats a deep navy blue, which offset the border of violet morning glories well.

A smiling blonde came over and greeted Kate. Her nametag read Stace, but somehow Kate would have pegged her for a McKenna fiancé without it. She had the kind of bright, happy personality that seemed to fit with what Kate knew of the McKenna men so far. "Welcome to the Morning Glory," Stace said. "Can I get you some coffee?"

"Sure." Kate put out her hand. "And if you have a sec, I'd love to chat with you. I'm Kate and I'm making your wedding cupcakes this week."

"Kate, how nice to finally meet you in person." The other woman smiled. "Brody told us about you. And so did Riley's grandmother. She said you made amazing chocolates."

"Thank you." Brody had been talking about her. At first, it flattered her, then she realized it made sense. He'd hired her to make Stace's wedding cake, after all, and giving her business a plug would be part of that. Kate had been puzzling over Brody's words from Saturday all weekend. Something troubled him, but what it was, she didn't know. He'd left the necklace behind, right next to a whole lot of unanswered questions.

"Listen, I need to get a couple orders on the tables, but then I should have a few minutes to sit and chat. I'll bring us coffee." Stace cast a glance toward the clock on the wall. "And knowing my husband-to-be, he'll be walking in those doors in about thirty seconds for his omelet fix, so you can meet Riley, too."

"Sounds great." Kate gave Stace a smile.

A few seconds later, the door opened and a man who looked like a younger version of Brody strode inside, straight to Stace. He took her in his arms, gave her a quick dip that had her laughing, then a longer kiss that had her blushing. She gave him a gentle swat, then gestured in Kate's direction.

Riley crossed the room, a wide smile on his face. He slid into the opposite seat and put out a hand. "Riley McKenna. The youngest and cutest McKenna brother—and you can tell Brody I said so."

Kate laughed and shook hands with Riley. She liked him from the start. "Nice to meet you. Kate Spencer, owner of Nora's Sweet Shop."

"So you're the one that has my brother all distracted. The man doesn't know if he's coming or going lately."

Had he said that? Been talking about her? "Brody and I are just working together. He's helping me out while my assistant is out of town."

"Well, for Brody it's more than some baking and measuring. The man can't stop talking about you." Riley leaned across the table. "He's smitten, I'd say. Though if you tell him I said that, I'll deny it."

Kate put up her hands. "Brody and I are not dating—" well, Saturday had been kind of a date, and the tension between them spoke of something more than friendship "—I'm not sure he's interested in me that way." Because despite the day they'd spent together, the flirting and the jokes, he kept taking two steps forward, one step back. The mixed signals confused her, and as much as she'd told Riley and Stace she'd come here to get more details for their wedding cake, she knew the truth. She'd stopped in to pump those who knew Brody best for more information. Something to help her solve the puzzle of the enigmatic Brody McKenna.

"Tell me," Riley said, "is Brody there pretty much every day?"

"Well, yes, but—"

"Is he doing nice things like opening the door for you?"

"Well, yes, but—"

"And is he finding excuses to run into you when he doesn't have to be there?"

"Well, yes, but—"

"Then he's interested. Trust me, Brody doesn't waste his time on things that don't matter to him. If he's around you all the time, he's interested. Not to mention, he manages to bring up your name about... oh, a hundred times in conversation."

Stace slid into the booth beside Riley and handed Kate a cup of coffee. "You talking about Brody?"

"Yup. And how the middle brother is the last to learn

that a good woman is the secret to happiness." Riley pressed a kiss to Stace's cheek. "It's always the smart ones that are the dumbest."

"I agree with that." Stace gave him a gentle nudge, then turned to Kate. "Riley was just as bad as Brody. Kept on pretending he didn't have any interest in me. And meanwhile, he was drooling behind my back."

Riley feigned horror. "I was not. That was Finn with Ellie."

Kate laughed. "Brody mentioned him a few times."

"The first to fall and get married, and he surprised the hell out of all of us by eloping. He's got one kid already, another on the way. By taking the plunge, he blazed the trail for the rest of us." Riley chuckled. "And this weekend, it'll be my turn. I can't wait."

Stace beamed at him. "Neither can I." Riley slipped his arm behind Stace and drew her a little closer, a little tighter.

Kate dug a notepad out of her purse. "While I have you two here, I wanted to ask you some questions about the cupcakes. Brody gave me information, but—"

"He's a guy and they aren't big on details, right?" Stace said. "Whatever Brody told you, though, is probably just fine. I'm the least fussy person you'll ever meet. Just make them edible and pretty and I'll be happy."

"Because all you want to do is marry me, right?" Riley said.

"No. All I want to do is gorge on cupcakes." She laughed. "Okay, and marry you."

Riley swiped a hand across his forehead. "Phew. You had me worried there for a minute. I thought the wedding was all an elaborate plot for dessert."

"Oh, it is," Stace said with a grin. "And you're the dessert I'm getting."

The two of them embodied happiness. Kate envied them a bit. No, a lot. Would she ever meet a man who would love her that much? "I'm not sure my cupcakes can live up to that," she said with a smile.

"I'm sure they'll be all that and more. I heard all about your chocolates from Mary at dinner last week."

"A family dinner that Brody skipped," Riley said. "I heard it was because he was working with you."

"I'm sorry, if I had known he should have been at a family dinner—"

Riley put up a hand to stop her. "It was no big deal, really. Honestly, we're all glad Brody started working with you. It's been good for him."

Stace nodded. Concern filled both their faces. "Be patient with Brody. He's been through a lot."

Did that explain the distance he maintained? The way he pulled back every time they got close? What could possibly be that bad that he felt he couldn't tell her?

"He told me his parents died." Kate shook her head. "I meant yours, Riley. I'm sorry about that."

"Thanks, but that isn't what troubles Brody these days. He's been through something…traumatic. In the recent past." Riley exchanged a glance with Stace.

Something Brody hadn't shared. The big thing he kept dancing around, then dropping? Hurt roared inside Kate. She had sat there with him and poured her heart out, sharing her deepest fears, and he had yet to do the same. Why?

"He said he's working with me because it helps him

get his mind off things," Kate said. "I'm glad that baking can do that for him."

And that he can avoid the hard topics yet coax them out of me.

"Brody hates to cook," Riley said with a laugh. "Like seriously runs the other way if someone turns on the oven. He's a takeout only man."

"Then why would he offer to help me?"

Again, Riley and Stace exchanged a glance and again, Kate got the feeling there was something— something big—they weren't telling her. "You need to ask him about that," Riley said. "Just know that if Brody is there doing the thing he hates the most in the world, there is a really, really big reason for him doing so."

"Bigger than your wedding?" Kate asked.

Riley thought a second. "Brody's not there for our wedding. He's there because—" Stace laid a hand on Riley's arm and he cut off the sentence. "Brody's a good man," Riley said instead. "And he's trying his damnedest to do the right thing. So before you judge him, think about that. And give him the benefit of the doubt."

Thursday afternoon, Brody sat in his office, surrounded by charts he needed to finish up and notes he should be reviewing, and ignored it all. He'd come so close to telling Kate the truth on Saturday, but at the last minute, chickened out, using the emergency as an excuse to get out of there. And in the days since, he'd found one excuse after another to avoid the bakery. Instead, he'd gone for long, hard, punishing runs that hadn't solved a damned thing.

The problem? He liked Kate. Liked her a lot. And he knew if he wanted a future with her, then he had to start being honest. Trust that she could handle the information, and not be worse for knowing it.

Andrew's concerns continued to nag in the back of Brody's head, though. Who would know her better than her brother? Maybe Andrew was right to protect her, or maybe he didn't realize his sister's strength.

How well did Brody know her, though, after only a couple weeks? Better than her own flesh and blood?

Mrs. Maguire gave his door a soft knock, and came inside. "Do you need anything else before I leave, Doctor?"

"No, thanks, Mrs. Maguire." His head nurse had been a model of efficiency this week, and kept him on track despite his uncharacteristic lack of attention to his practice. She'd noticed, and mentioned it a few times. He'd attributed his inattentiveness to exhaustion, an excuse that didn't work, given he'd worked half days all week.

She lingered in the doorway, then came inside and put a hand on the back of his visitor's chair but didn't sit. "I've noticed you've been troubled lately, Doc." He put up a hand to argue, but she cut him off. "Can I give you some advice? The same advice Doc Watkins gave me one day?"

Concern etched her features. Working side by side with him for years had given Mrs. Maguire an insight into what made Brody tick. Maybe she'd share something that could take the edge off his emotions, give him a way to find his direction again. "Sure."

She swung around to the front of the chair and eased into it. "Did I ever tell you about my daughter, Sharon?"

"Just that she's married and given you two, no, three grandchildren to spoil." Every day it seemed Mrs.

Maguire put out a new picture of one of the three kids on her desk. Or a new drawing colored with thick crayons, and marked with love for Grandma. The kids lived a couple towns over, and Brody knew Mrs. Maguire devoted every spare minute to seeing them.

A smile curved across Mrs. Maguire's face. "She has indeed. But for a time there, I didn't think she was going to do anything with her life, anything except die."

As far as he could remember, Mrs. Maguire had only shared the good news about her family, never any kind of troubles beyond the typical colds or restaurant meltdowns. "I didn't know that. What happened?"

"This was before your time, and back when it was just me and Doc Watkins. As a single mom, I juggled everything—work, school, soccer matches. Sharon felt neglected, I think. When she got to high school, she made a lot of bad choices. Fell in with the wrong crowd. Pot led to coke, led to crack. In those days, crack ran rampant." She shook her head. "I thought I was going to lose her. I did everything I could to try to keep her safe. Console her, stay home with her, whatever it took to keep her on track. But nothing worked. One day at a time, I watched my baby die."

"Oh, Mrs. Maguire, I'm so sorry." He couldn't imagine the stress on her shoulders during those days, coupled with working full-time and paying the bills.

"And here I was, a nurse. The kind of person who should know better, you know? I kept trying to fix it, like putting a band-aid on a cut, but it wasn't a cut, it was a hemorrhage, and she didn't want the help."

"What did you do?"

"I came in here one day and I cried to Doc Watkins. Told him I had to quit so I could take care of my baby.

I was going to devote myself full time to trying to fix Sharon. And you know what he told me?"

Brody shook his head.

"He said if I quit, it would be the worst thing I could do. Well, he said more than that, and a whole lot more colorfully than I would. You know Doc Watkins. He was nothing if not direct."

Brody chuckled. "I remember."

Mrs. Maguire crossed her hands in her lap and dropped her gaze to her fingers. "Back then, there wasn't a lot of that fanciness about enabling and co-dependency, but that's what it was. I just didn't see it. All I saw was that I was protecting my daughter, helping her. Doc gave me the number of a great rehab. Told me to drop her off and drive away. I did, but damn, I didn't want to. She was crying and screaming and calling me names, then begging me to come back in the same breath. I had to shut the windows, turn the rear-view mirror, so I wouldn't give in." Tears filled the older woman's eyes at the memory, and she leaned forward, grabbed a tissue from the box on his desk, and dabbed at her face. "I left her there. Hardest damned thing I ever did in my life, and also the best. Three months later, she came out clean. Moved to Brookline, got herself a job in a dress shop, and after a year or so, met the man that became her husband."

"I'm glad that all worked out." He'd admired Mrs. Maguire before, but his esteem for her increased ten-fold. The woman sitting across from him possessed an incredible inner strength. "You must have been so worried."

"I was, but more than that, I was beating myself up for not fixing it. It took me a long time to realize that

some things are out of my hands. I couldn't make her
come clean. I couldn't make her want it; she had to
want it for herself. Just because I have medical training doesn't make me a miracle worker." She crumpled
the tissue into her fist, then leaned forward. "Most of
all, I had to learn that sometimes, you just have to cut
yourself some slack. You and me both."

"I try, Mrs. Maguire. I really do."

"No, you don't. I've seen your face ever since you
got back from Afghanistan. Whatever happened over
there, you are blaming yourself for and now that weight
has become an albatross around your neck." She put up
a hand. "Now I don't know the whole story, and I might
be just talking out of my hat, but all I can say is that I
have been in shoes similar to yours, and if you put your
faith in others, and stop beating yourself up for what
you can't control, what you couldn't fix, it'll all work
out. You are a doctor, and you're used to fixing, ban-
daging. Not everything can be fixed. Some things just
have to be." She got to her feet, and smoothed a hand
down her jacket. "I've said my piece, and I'll let you
be. I'm not trying to tell you what to do, Dr. McKenna,
just trying to offer you a solution. Take it if you want."
She gave him a kind smile, then left the room.

Brody got to his feet and went to the window. He
looked out at the busy streets of Newton, beginning to
fill with cars now that the clock had ticked past five.
For the next few hours, it would be bumper to bumper with people trying to get home to their lives, their
homes, their families. They would sit around the table
and talk about their days, and few, if any, would realize just how lucky they were to be together.

He thought of Mrs. Maguire and her daughter, and

how close his head nurse had come to losing her only child. He thought of albatrosses and choices, and after a long time, he pulled out the card, read it over for the millionth time, then tucked it back into his wallet. It was time he told Kate the real story about her brother.

And let the chips fall where they may after that.

CHAPTER NINE

KATE had baked and decorated, frosted and sugared. But it hadn't been enough to make her forget what Riley and Stace had said. Or to put Brody McKenna out of her mind.

Because she'd started to like him. He kept his cards close to his chest—heck, hidden inside his chest—but every once in a while, the other side of Brody peeked out. A playful, sweet side. Like when they'd danced together at the rest home. When he'd dug in and started baking, even wearing the pink apron. At the same time, he showed this dimension of caring. Like the kind of man a woman could lean against, depend upon. Even if being around him stirred her in a way she hadn't been stirred before.

Would it be worth it to take the risk and fall in love with him? Or would she be burned by a man who was keeping part of himself hidden? She'd seen her mother do it time and again with her father. Giving, giving, giving, and never receiving his full heart in return. Would Brody be the same? Would she be repeating her mother's mistakes?

Her conversation with Riley and Stace had only stirred the pot. What had Brody been hiding behind those blue eyes? The flame of Brody McKenna drew her again and again. She needed to exercise caution—or she'd get burned.

"Somebody's got a lot on her mind."

Kate jerked her head up and looked at her grandmother. "Huh?"

"You just turned that rose into a radish." She pointed at the red clump of buttercream on top of the cupcake.

"Oh, no." She swiped the ruined decoration off, then set down the piping bag. "I guess I am a little distracted."

"And I know why." Nora hefted a heavy tub of frosting onto the counter and started to peel off the lid.

"Grandma, quit that!" Kate said, sliding in to finish the job before her grandmother hurt herself. "No helping."

"You need the help. I have the experience. Let me give you a hand."

Kate sighed. She knew her grandmother. She wouldn't give up. "Okay. If you promise to take it easy, and sit down while you work, can you frost those cupcakes over there?"

Nora laughed. "You sound like you're the grandmother and I'm the granddaughter."

"Just watching out for my favorite grandma." Kate slid a stool over to the counter, then plopped a platter of red devil cupcakes and a piping bag of cream cheese frosting in front of her grandmother. She laid a hand on Nora's shoulder. "Thanks, Grandma."

Nora took Kate's hand and gave it a squeeze. "Anytime, sweetie. I love this place almost as much as I love you."

"Ditto." She grinned, then dipped her head to focus

on assembling the order she'd been working on. Maybe talking about work would keep her from thinking about Brody. "By the way, I looked at that second location the other day."

"You did? What'd you think of it?"

"It was…perfect. In this quaint little town square in Weymouth, across the street from an old-fashioned movie theater. There's a florist and a café nearby, and a hospital right down the street."

"I don't think it gets much better than that," Nora said. "Did you make an offer?"

"Not yet."

"What are you waiting for?"

Kate shrugged, then threw up her hands. "I don't know. A sign? A big, blinking, this is the right decision to make sign."

Nora laughed. "Life never gives us those. If it did, every choice we make would be easy as pie."

"True."

Nora laid a hand on her granddaughter's shoulder. "You'll know the right answer when the time comes. Meanwhile, you have a big night tonight. Are you ready?"

Kate glanced down at the dress she'd put on, the heels she'd brought to work just for tonight. "As ready as I'll ever be. If I just stick with the desserts, I'll be fine. Either way, I'm packing tissues in my purse."

Her grandmother gave her a quick hug. "Such a smart, practical girl. No wonder I'm so proud of you."

The bell over the door rang, and Kate turned to go out to the shop when she heard Brody's voice call out a hello. Her heart tripped, and a smile curved across her face. Not thinking about Brody had worked for, oh, five seconds.

"Hmm…and you wonder why you're distracted," Nora said. "I think the reason just walked in."

"It has nothing to do with him," Kate whispered. "Nothing at all."

"Mmm, hmm." Nora drew a little frosting heart on the stainless steel counter. Kate swiped the romantic symbol onto her finger and plopped the sweet treat in her mouth before Brody walked in and saw it.

Damn. Every time she saw Brody McKenna, she forgot to breathe. He had on a suit jacket with his shirt and tie today, and he looked so handsome she could have fainted. "Hi," she said, because her brain wouldn't process any other words.

"Hi, yourself." He started to shrug out of the jacket. He had a tall, lean body, defined in all the right places. His muscles rippled under the pressed cotton of his shirt, and she wondered what he'd look like bare-chested. She'd seen him in a T-shirt and shorts and that had been a delicious sight that had lingered in her mind. What would he look like, wet from the shower? Fresh out of bed in the morning? In the dark of night, slipping under the sheets?

Damn. Why did this man affect her so?

"Uh, you might want to keep that on," she said, putting up a hand to stop him. "I have another delivery tonight. I forgot to tell you earlier. If you don't mind helping me, there'll be a free dinner in it for you."

"A free dinner? One that doesn't come out of a microwave or a drive-through? Who can turn down that offer?" He grinned, then entered the kitchen.

Her stomach flipped, her heart tripped, and she knew

why her thoughts lingered on him whenever they were apart. That smile. And those eyes. And everything else about him. In that second, she decided she'd take the risk, open her heart.

"Hello, Mrs. Spencer," he said to Kate's grandmother.

"Why hello, Dr. McKenna. So nice to see you again."

"You, too, ma'am."

"Why, would you look at the time?" Nora said. She took off her apron, and laid it beside the piping bag. "I completely forgot I promised your grandfather I'd go out with him for the early birds dinner special tonight. I better go." She shrugged into her coat. "You two can handle this alone, can't you?"

She laid a slight emphasis on the word "alone" and gave her granddaughter a knowing smile. Behind Brody's back, she drew a heart in the air and pointed at Kate. "Oh, and, Brody," Nora said, "I'd love to have you over for Wednesday night dinner at our house next week."

"I'd be honored, Mrs. Spencer. Thank you."

"Good. I'll see you at six. Kate knows the address." She gave her granddaughter a smile. "Maybe she'll even drive you."

Kate had no doubt her grandmother would drive over and pick up Brody herself if her granddaughter didn't. Matchmaker Nora at work again. Andrew had had some of those tendencies himself, always telling Kate he'd keep an eye out for the perfect man for his amazing sister.

"Do you need me to bring anything?" Brody asked.

"Aren't you sweet? No, nothing at all. Just bring yourself." Nora shot Kate another smile of approval for Brody. He'd racked up several brownie points and had clearly moved to the top of Nora's list. "That'll be enough."

Nora headed out the door. Kate wished the floor would open up and swallow her but it didn't. Or a customer would come in and save her from the awkward silence. None did. Or the sky would fall and create a distraction—

None of that happened. Instead, the room became a warm, tight space of just her. And Brody. Her gaze roamed over him. Desire pulsed in her veins. He wore a half smile, and in an odd way, that turned her on more than a full smile. She wanted to feel his hard chest beneath her palms, but most of all, she wanted to kiss him.

Why had he yet to make a move in that direction? Brody didn't strike her as the shy type. She had read attraction between them, she was sure of it. What was holding him back from pushing this further?

She watched him loading the finished cupcakes into boxes, and read tension in his shoulders, a distance in his words, his smile. She kept on talking, filling the room with endless chatter, if only to keep from asking the obvious question—

What's wrong?

They worked together for several minutes, exchanging small talk about their days. The whole thing seemed so ordinary, smacking of a domestic life with Brody. She could imagine a future like this—her coming home from the shop, sitting across the dinner table from him, and talking about everything, and nothing at all. Like ordinary couples with ordinary lives.

Already, that told her that her heart had connected

with him. A lot. She was falling for him. But the falling felt nice, like tumbling into a warm pool.

As much as she wanted to linger in that pool, she held back, because she sensed a reservation in Brody. Maybe he didn't feel the same way. Maybe he did, as though it was moving too fast. Or maybe she had read him wrong. And she could be making the mistake of a lifetime.

"There, that's the last one," she said, sandwiching the last cupcake in the container. She closed the lid and handed it to Brody. He stacked them together, then gave her a grin.

"Another job done."

"Yep." Joanne would be back Saturday, and then her afternoons of working with Brody would come to an end. Already, she could see that finish line, and it saddened her. She'd gotten used to having him here.

"I'm sorry about my grandmother earlier," Kate said, "but you don't have to go to dinner if you don't want." Her roundabout way of saying *if you aren't interested in me, here's your out.*

"I'd love to go. Your grandmother didn't bother me at all by asking me over. I think there's something in a grandmother's DNA that makes them bound and determined to matchmake," Brody said. "When I saw mine a few days ago, she said the same thing. That I should bring you to the next family dinner, which in case I get in trouble for not inviting you, is at Mary McKenna's house in Newton, on Sunday at two. She's just a few blocks north of here."

Kate laughed. "Seems like our grandmothers are determined to bring us together."

"Mine heard glowing reports from Riley about how

nice you were. And that got her wheels turning, thinking that you and I..." His voice trailed off.

"Yeah, my grandmother, too." Kate let out a nervous
laugh. She brushed at her hair. Damn. She was acting
like a schoolgirl. Her face heated under Brody's lingering gaze. She turned away to grab a spoon and moved
too fast, unnerved by the tension, by the unanswered
questions. Did he like her? Or not?

As she pivoted, her arm bumped the bowl, and sent
it tumbling onto the floor. When it hit the concrete, the
violet frosting in the bowl splattered upward, and out-
ward, spreading in a burst of color on Brody's shirt and
his suit jacket. "Oh no! I'm sorry."

"No problem. I've had worse on my shirt. Especially
during flu season." He slipped off the jacket, then, just
like in her fantasy, he began to undo the buttons. Her
heart skipped a beat, and nearly stopped when he peeled
apart the panels of his shirt and revealed, a lean, muscled chest.

Oh. My. God. Kate opened her mouth. Closed it
again. "Uh...I can get you a T-shirt. If you don't mind
one that says Nora's Sweet Shop."

"Better to wear the words than the actual sweets."
Brody grinned.

Kate spun away before she reached out and ran a
hand down his chest. Or worse. Like threw him onto
the stainless steel counter and ravaged his body. She
grabbed a T-shirt from the glass case out front and
brought it back with her. "At least this is brown, instead of pink like the aprons."

"It's almost manly. Thanks."

"Anytime." And anytime he wanted to take his shirt

off in her presence, he could. But she didn't say that, either.

He moved closer, standing inches away now, that broad chest so close she could feel the heat against her own skin. "Do you, uh, want to give it to me?"

Way to go, Kate, hold the man's shirt hostage.

"Oh. Oh, yes. I'm sorry. I…got distracted." She inhaled, and caught the woodsy scent of his cologne. Dark, mysterious, like wandering a forest in the middle of the night.

"Distracted by what?"

"You." There. The truth hung there, in plain sight. "You distract me, Brody McKenna."

"I don't mean to." He reached up a hand and cupped her jaw. His hand was big, strong, yet gentle against her skin. "I keep telling myself not to do this, not to take things further, but then every time I leave here, all I do is think about you. And when I'm near you, all I can do is think about kissing you."

"Really?" She swallowed. "But…"

"But what?"

"But…you haven't."

A smile curved across his face. Slow, sexy. "No, I haven't. And maybe it's time I remedied that."

"Maybe it is."

"Do you want me to kiss you, Kate?"

"Yes." She exhaled. "Yes, I do."

"Good." He leaned in, winnowing the gap between them until a fraction of space separated them. Her pulse rumbled like thunder and a craving for Brody grew inside her until the world disappeared.

She watched the gold flecks dance in his eyes. Her heart stuttered, stopped, stuttered again.

"Ah, Kate…" he said, her name a harsh whisper, then he closed the space and kissed her.

His lips were hard against hers at first, a strong, wild kiss, like a sudden summer storm. His hands tangled in her hair, and he pulled her to him, tight against his chest. She curved into Brody, heat racing through her body, charging up her spine. Her hands worked against his back, feeling the ripple of the muscles she had fantasized about. The warm expanse of his skin, the hard places of his body. He plundered her mouth, his tongue dancing hot and furious with hers.

She couldn't think. Couldn't breathe. Couldn't move. Desire pounded a hard rhythm in her body, and for a long, long second she forgot where she was. She only knew Brody was kissing her and it was the sexiest, most exquisite experience of her life. She shifted against him, pressing her pelvis to his erection, wanting more, wanting—

Brody broke away. He cursed and spun toward the window. "I'm sorry, Kate. I shouldn't have done that. I wasn't thinking. I…"

She laid a hand on his bare shoulder and waited until he'd pivoted back to face her. "It's okay, Brody. I wanted that as much as you did."

"I know, but… I need to talk to you before we take this any further."

The clock chimed the half hour. She cursed the timing. "Can it wait? We have to get going before we're late. Already, with the traffic and set up time, we're likely to barely make it there before the event starts."

"Yeah, it can wait." He drew the T-shirt over his head, and she bit back a sigh of disappointment. "A little while, but not too long, okay?"

"Sounds serious." She grinned. "You're not giving me a fatal diagnosis, Doctor, are you?"

"No, no." He fiddled with the stack of orders on the counter beside him. "Just something I've been meaning to tell you."

"Okay." She lifted the boxes of cupcakes, then placed them in his arms. Curiosity piqued inside her but she had to concentrate on work for now. Like he said, they'd talk later. "We'd better head out now or we'll be late."

"If you don't mind, we can stop by my office. I keep an extra shirt and tie there, for accidents just like this."

"Sure." He helped her load the cupcakes into the van, repeating what they had done two nights before, with her driving, him sitting in the passenger's seat. They drove the few blocks to his office, and Kate waited in the van while he went inside and traded the T-shirt for a clean shirt and suit jacket. When he returned, she put the van in gear.

Brody glanced over at her. "You look beautiful."

"Thank you." She smoothed a hand over the black jersey fabric of the sweetheart neckline dress she'd chosen. "This is a special event."

"Big one for Nora's Sweet Shop?"

"You could say that." She paused. "Really, it's a big one for me."

"Sounds important."

"It is. It's a way of thanking the people who have been there for me when I needed them." She glanced over at him. "It's a thank you for the troops."

He tensed beside her. Whatever he'd been holding back seemed to be bubbling under the surface. Why?

"Is something bothering you?" she asked.

He glanced out the window, as they headed out of

Newton and into the city, against the flow of outgoing traffic. Horns honked. Lights flashed. But Kate's attention stayed on Brody.

"Yes and no," he said after a while.

"You want to talk about it?"

He didn't say anything for a long time, so long she thought he hadn't heard the question. Finally, he let out a breath. "I've been wrestling with something for some time now and I know I need to talk about it, but…" he shook his head, "doing so is a lot harder than I expected." He paused again, and she waited for him to continue. "The last medical mission trip I took was really difficult. I lost a patient, and it's been haunting me."

"Oh, Brody, I'm sorry."

"I made a promise to the patient, one I'm not so sure I can keep anymore. He didn't want me to say what happened to him. He just wanted me to encourage someone very close to him to focus on the future, not on what happened in the past, and I just don't know if that's the right thing to do." Brody hesitated again and then looked at her. "If it were you, what would you want?"

She thought about her answer. "I don't know. A part of me feels like I've just started moving forward, and knowing more, or going back there would be like the day I found out. I just…don't want to go there again. I'm just getting out of that cement, you know?"

"So you're saying it would be better not to know?"

"For me, for now…that's what I'd want. Maybe down the road, it would be easier."

"Thanks for the advice. I'll keep that in mind." He turned to the window, and watched the world go by, a clear sign the subject was closed.

The sun had started to set, casting a golden lake over the rippling green waters of Boston Harbor, and twinkling halos over every skyscraper.

"The city is amazing, isn't it?" Kate said. "Every winter, I say I want to move and open up a location in Florida or Hawaii, or any place that doesn't get snow. But there's just something about Boston, something... magical, that I love. No matter where I go, my heart will always be here."

"I feel the same way. I've traveled all over the country, seen a lot of the world, and there's still nothing like Boston. I love it here, for all its faults...and traffic."

Kate laughed. "Yeah, the traffic is one thing I can do without. My grandparents don't mind it. They say it gives them extra alone time in the car. They're old romantics that way."

"They sound it." Brody glanced out the window, watching the city go by in a blur of buildings. "I guess everyone hopes to find a true love like that, the kind that can last a lifetime. I know my grandparents were like that. My parents, not so much. They fought all the time. Then they'd make up, and it'd be fiery in a different way. I think they were two opposite souls, who just couldn't let go of each other."

"Sometimes the fireworks are good." Though for her parents, attraction hadn't been enough to sustain their marriage. They'd been too different to make it work, too infatuated to slow down and think before they tied the knot.

Still, fireworks summed up what had been going on inside her ever since she'd met Brody. And every time he smiled at her. Or touched her. And, oh, yes, when he kissed her.

Fireworks. Bottle rockets—no, Roman candles—of desire, launching in her chest. Fireworks alone didn't create a relationship, and she needed to remember that.

Brody had turned his attention on her, and it took all her effort to keep her eyes on the road and not on him. "Is that what you're looking for? The fireworks and happiness, even in a traffic jam?"

She sighed. "I gave up on that a long time ago. My parents were like yours. All fireworks, no substance. I guess watching their marriage disintegrate made me lose faith in ever finding Mr. Right."

"And who is your Mr. Right?"

"Why, are you applying for the job?" She cast him a grin, pretending the question was a joke. But after that kiss, a part of her hoped like hell the answer was yes.

"Can't do that if I don't know the qualifications." He grinned. "I could be all wrong for you."

"Could be." Or he could be all right. She didn't know yet, but a part of her really wanted to find out. "I guess my brother is the one I hold up as the ideal for all the men I meet. Andrew was smart, and funny, and driven, and above all, a hero. The kind of man who was true to those he loved, loyal to everyone he knew, and braver than anyone in the world. You could count on him to be honest, to be the one you depended on, rather than him depending on you."

"He sounds like the perfect guy."

She laughed. "Oh, he was far from perfect, believe me. There was a time when we were little, like nine and seven. He and I were fighting over a toy, and he slugged me, hard. My eye swelled up, my cheek turned purple, and he felt so bad, he carried me to my grandmother, and stood over me for hours, changing out the ice pack and worrying like a new mother. He got in a lot of trouble that day, and for years, would tell me how bad he felt about it. I, of course, being the evil older sister, milked that injury for all I could."

Brody laughed. "I know that trick. Riley and I have given Finn a hard time and taken him on a guilt trip more than once."

"I've met Riley and I can see that about him. He seems like he was...mischievous as a child."

Brody laughed. "He still is."

"What's Finn like?"

"The total opposite of Riley. Finn is an architect, all straight lines and organizational charts, although marrying Ellie and adopting a child has loosened him up a lot. Riley runs an after school program at Wilmont Academy. He was the slowest to grow up, but he's making us all proud now."

"And you, of course, being a doctor who also volunteers his time to help the needy. You must make them all proud, too."

His gaze went to the window again. For a long time, he was silent, just watching the traffic go by, the houses yield to skyscrapers. "Some days I think I do. Other days...not so much."

He didn't elaborate and she didn't press. Once again, Brody had closed a door between them, and Kate reminded herself she didn't need a man like that. At its heart, this wasn't a relationship, it was a business deal. He was helping her and in exchange, he'd get the cupcakes for Riley's wedding. Fireworks or not, if there was no substance, there wasn't anything to build on.

Then why did she care what troubles lay behind those blue eyes? Why did she keep pressing for more?

Because she sensed something good, deep inside of Brody. Something worth fighting for.

"So, who's your ideal Mrs. Right?" she asked, up-ending her own vow to stay neutral. She exited the highway, and came to stop at a red light. A sign for her and Brody? "The perfect doctor's wife with the gloves and pillbox hat?"

"Lord, no, that would drive me nuts." He chuckled. "I'm not that formal. Ever. I like women who are... natural."

"As in no makeup, wearing sandals and T-shirts?" The light turned green, and Kate accelerated again.

"As in they act like themselves all the time. I hate when people act one way but feel the opposite. I don't like secrets or surprises."

"Me, too. If you asked me my relationship deal-breaker, it would be dishonesty. I can't stand being lied to. Have the courage to tell me the truth, or don't waste my time." She flicked on her directional, then pulled into the hotel's parking garage. The van bumped over a speed strip. Kate cast a quick glance at the cargo, but nothing had moved. "If you want people who are true to their word and to those they care about, then you've come to the right place tonight."

Brody didn't say much as they pulled the boxes out of the van, then loaded them onto a cart and headed up the to the third floor in the hotel elevator. Once inside the ballroom, a hotel staffer directed Kate to the banquet table, telling her to set up dessert on the far corner.

She glanced at Brody several times, but the easy banter between them had disappeared. Had she said something wrong? Or was he still thinking about the patient he had lost?

"We only have a few minutes before everyone arrives, so we need to hurry," she said. They worked out an assembly line of sorts, with Brody handing Kate the cupcakes while she laid them on tiered trays she had brought with her.

"Red, white and blue?" he said, noting the arrangement of the desserts. "It almost looks like you've made flags."

"I did." She pointed to the array of cupcakes, set in the familiar pattern of the flag for the USA. Then she drew in a deep breath. Tonight would be difficult, no doubt, but the cause was a worthy one, and Kate vowed to suck it up and not cry. "Okay. Here they come."

The ballroom doors opened and dozens of men and women in uniform strode into the ballroom, chatting in low tones as the band took up the stage and began to play "America the Beautiful." The room filled with a sea of green and camouflage, flanked by bright flags on either end.

"I haven't seen these people in a long time. I'm so nervous and excited."

"I thought you said it was a thank you," Brody said.

"It is." She leaned in and lowered her voice. "For the members of Andrew's unit, along with several other units from Massachusetts who returned to the States in the last few weeks. It was originally supposed to be a retirement party for the top ranking general in the area, but the general put up his own money and paid to have a party for the troops instead. So it mushroomed into this big event. They came to me for the cupcakes because they knew my brother had..." She bit her lip and shook her head. She would not cry tonight. Would not. "Well, that he didn't come home."

The troops settled into chairs that ringed tables decorated with patriotic colors. An honor guard marched in, raised the flag, and the whole room stood at attention to sing "The Star Spangled Banner."

"There are members of Andrew's unit here tonight?" Brody hung back behind the banquet tables with Kate, his stomach riding his throat.

"Yes. I can't wait to introduce you to them."

Introduce him? The thought hit Brody in the chest like an anvil. Kate had said the one thing she couldn't abide was someone who didn't tell the truth. All Brody had done since he met her was lie. Lie about who he was. Lie about why he was in her shop. Lie about his volunteer work. He'd done it because it had been Andrew's last request, but now…

Now he wasn't sure it had been the right decision. How could he expect her to move forward, to look to the future, if Brody was holding a key to her past in his hands?

"These are the true heroes," she whispered to Brody. Tears filled her eyes, while she watched the general take the stage and thank the brave men and women who had given their lives in defense of their country. "The people who risked everything for those back home."

Brody had thought he was doing the right thing by not telling Kate about Andrew's death, but he'd been wrong. The woman beside him was no daisy. She was as strong as an oak tree, and the time had come for him to tell her the truth. He'd be there to help her through it, and she would be okay. He'd make sure of it.

The general finished his speech, then began introducing the vendors who had donated their time and products to the event. "And I'd also like to introduce

Miss Kate Spencer, owner of Nora's Sweet Shop. She lost her brother, Andrew, in Afghanistan last month. A tragic accident, that occurred while Andrew and members of his team were accompanying a medical team helping local villagers. Kate, come on up here." The general waved to her.

She hesitated. "I don't know if I'm ready for this," she whispered. She spun toward Brody. "Go with me? At least until the stage?"

"Of course." He took her hand, and they walked across the room and over to the stage. Kate gave Brody a smile, then climbed the few steps and crossed to the podium. "Thank you, General Martin. I'm afraid you've given me too much credit. I didn't do anything but make cupcakes. It's all of you who made the sacrifices and gave of yourselves. I hope these desserts thank you, at least in some tiny measure, for all you have done. I know my brother was proud to be in the National Guard, but not as proud as I was to call him my brother."

A roar of applause and hearty agreement went up from the crowd. Kate gave them all a smile, then climbed back down the stairs and took Brody's hand again. "Thank you."

"You did great." She'd been poised and brief, and delivered a speech that touched people with a few words. He'd never seen another woman who could do so much, and touch so many, so easily.

Damn, he liked her. A lot.

And because he did, he would tell her who he really was, and what had happened in that dusty hut, and pray it all worked out. In his practice, he'd seen a thousand times that the truth gave patients power. To make their own decisions, to handle a diagnosis. Kate needed that, and Brody was done waiting to give it to her.

"I'm just glad I got through it without crying." She smiled again, but this time her eyes shimmered. "It's still hard to talk about him sometimes."

"I understand. More than you know." He led her through the crowd and toward the banquet tables. Maybe they could slip out for a few minutes and he could talk to her. Or maybe it would be better to wait until they had left, and they could find a quiet place to talk alone.

Along the way, several troops got to their feet to offer condolences, and thank-yous for the cupcakes. Brody's feet sputtered to a stop when a familiar face rose to greet Kate. "Hey, Kate. Nice to see you again."

"Artie! Oh my gosh, it's been so long since I've seen you!" She let go of Brody's hand and gave the tall man a big hug. "How have you been?"

Artie Gavins, one of the other men in Andrew's unit. Brody forgot what his job had been, but he knew his face. He'd bandaged it the same day that Andrew had died. A serious man, who the others had dubbed "Straight Line" because he rarely cracked a smile. Andrew said Artie kept them all on track, but had also respected the other man's common sense approach.

"Fine, just fine," Artie said. Then his gaze traveled past Kate, and landed on Brody. It took him a second, but Brody could see him making the connection in his brain, processing the man in the suit jacket and tie, and connected him with the doctor in a khaki coat and jeans that he'd known last month. "Doc? Wow, I can't believe it's you. Hell, I almost didn't recognize you all dressed up and wearing a suit and tie."

Brody put out his hand and shook with the other man. "Good to see you, too."

And it was. There'd been so many wounded that day, so many to tend to. Seeing one of the men as hearty and hale as ever, gave Brody more reward than any paycheck ever could.

Still, he prayed Artie wouldn't say anything else. Brody didn't want Kate to find out who he was like this. He wanted time to explain it to her, time to get the words right, and here, in a public place, among all these people, wasn't the right place or time. "We, uh, better get back to the dessert table," he said to Kate. "I think we forgot to unload one of the boxes."

"Oh, yes, we need to get that done. Wouldn't want anyone to miss out on dessert." She gave Artie's shoulder a squeeze. "We'll catch up later."

"We will. Nice to see you, Kate, Doc." Artie took his seat again.

Brody hurried through the rest of the crowd with Kate, and back over to the banquet table. He wanted to pull Kate aside, but they were pinned in by the banquet tables and people were already lining up for food. No discreet way to duck out of the room.

"I didn't know you knew Artie," she said. "What a small world. How did you meet him?"

"He was…my patient once." Brody cast a glance down the long white tableclothed space. The hungry crowd was closing the gap between the chicken cordon bleu and dessert.

"Wow, and you remember him? That's pretty impressive, Doc."

"There are certain patients I never forget." Understatement of the year. "Listen, can we get out of here? I really want to talk to you."

"I can't leave. I promised the general I'd stay and eat with the troops. Plus, I'd love to catch up with Andrew's unit. It makes me feel closer to him. Why don't you stay? I promise, none of them bite." She grinned.

"I...I can't. I..." How could he explain it? The gap had closed, and the diners were now ten feet away. In that crowd was Artie, and most like Sully and Richards, the other two who had been on that mission with Andrew, also wounded, also part of the mad rush between Brody and the other doctor to save lives. "I...I need to talk to you, Kate."

She put a hand on his arm "Are you okay? You look...pale."

He glanced at the troops heading toward them, then at the woman who had just talked about the one army man who wouldn't be coming home, and the guilt hit him again in a wave so hard, he had to take a breath before he spoke again. "No, I'm not okay. Not at all."

"What is it?"

Andrew's last words rushed over Brody. *Don't tell her. She'll only grieve more.*

But that bequest warred with everything Brody knew to be true. A patient couldn't mend if they were in the dark about their ailment. Kate's heart was hurting her, and keeping the truth from her even one second longer wasn't going to help her heal. No amount of cupcake baking or location scouting could do what the simple truth could.

He was standing in a room with the bravest people in the world, and standing across from one of the bravest women he had ever met. He was doing her a disservice by keeping this tucked inside one minute longer. "Remember I told you about that patient I lost when I was on the medical mission?"

"Uh-huh." She pivoted a cupcake to the right, straightened another, until the frostings were aligned and the colors made straight lines in the flag design.

"That patient was someone you know."

She jerked her head up. "Someone I know?"

The hungry troops had reached the cupcakes. They exclaimed over the design as they selected one and moved on. "We need to go somewhere private, Kate."

"What, now?"

"Yes. It can't wait any longer. In fact, what I have to tell you shouldn't have waited as long as it has."

"Kate, I've saved a seat at the head table for you," the general said. "Come on and join me for dinner."

She glanced at Brody then back at the general. "I will, sir. Can you give me one second, please?"

The general nodded. "Take all the time you need."

She grabbed Brody's hand and they scooted along the wall, and out of the ballroom. Kate glanced back at the room as the doors shut. "I only have a minute, Brody."

He reached into his pocket and pulled out his wallet. Then he withdrew the card he had carried for so long and handed it to her. A parade of emotions washed over her face. Confusion, shock, hurt.

"How…how did you get this?" she asked.

The moment had come, and dread rumbled in Brody's gut. How he wished he didn't have to tell her this, didn't have to watch the happiness dim in her eyes. "Artie knows me…because I was his doctor."

"You said that."

"I was his doctor in Afghanistan. In fact, I treated several of the troops in that room."

"Wait. You were in Afghanistan? When?"

He let out a long breath. "I was part of a medical team that was going from village to village, helping provide care to people too poor or too far from a doctor, and also tending to those who had been injured because of the war. A National Guard unit had been dispatched to serve as protection for us because it was still a dangerous area." He met her gaze. "It was Andrew's unit, Kate."

"I don't understand. How did you know my brother? Is that how you got my card?"

"Remember that town I told you about? The one with the mountain range? We were there for several days and while we were, Andrew received one of your care packages."

She clutched the card tighter, her face pale. "I sent him those baskets every week, like clockwork. Lord only knows how the military got them to him, but they did."

"He loved those baskets." Brody chuckled a little at the memory of big, strong Andrew, as happy as a kid on Christmas when he received a box from home. He'd handed out cupcakes to all, boasting about his sister as he did. "I know he kidded you about them, but he kept every card, and talked about you all the time. When I met you, I felt like I already knew you."

"He talked about me?"

He nodded. "He was a good guy, your brother. Really good. It was probably a boring detail, just going from town to town with a couple doctors, but he treated it like the most important mission he had ever been on."

A smile wavered on her face. "That was Andrew. His whole life was about taking care of other people."

"He did a good job at it," Brody said.

"That still doesn't explain why *you* have the card I sent him."

Brody let out a long breath. He crossed to the brick wall and laid his palm against the cold, hard stone. The words stuck in his throat, churned with bile in his gut, but still he pressed forward. "I got to know your brother while he was with our group. We talked a lot. We had a lot in common, you know, both being from around here, and both being Red Sox fans and…"

"That's good. I'm glad he made a friend." Her voice broke a little.

"He was my friend," Brody said, turning to Kate. "I need you to know that. I cared about him a lot. And I wanted to save him. So badly, I really did."

"What do you mean?"

In the room behind them, the party rolled on. Someone laughed at a joke, and the band shifted into a pop song. Forks clanked, voices hummed.

Brody bit his lip. Damn. "All he ever talked about was you, and this shop, and getting back here to help his family out. He loved all of you very much, and he wanted nothing more than to see a chain of Nora's Sweet Shops someday. He told me you'd be scared to death to do it alone, but I should encourage you to go after your dreams. He worried about you. Worried that you'd get scared, or be too overwhelmed by his death, to keep going forward." Brody swallowed hard. Forced the words out. "He wanted me to make sure you did that. It was his dying wish."

"You…you were with him when he died?"

Brody nodded. He wanted to look away when he said the next part, but Kate deserved the truth, deserved the unvarnished, painful as hell truth. So he met her gaze, and said it. "I was his doctor."

"His doctor?" She pressed a hand to her forehead. "When were you going to tell me?"

"I tried to. A thousand times. But I didn't..." He sighed. "I didn't want to hurt you."

"You took care of him?"

"He was badly injured, and so were several other guys. That blast...it hurt them all. Some worse than others. The second doctor on the team was overwhelmed, less experienced, and there was a lot to deal with, all at once. It was chaos, Kate, sheer chaos. I did my best, believe me, but his injuries were too severe."

The words hung in the air between them for a long, long time. He watched her process them, her eyes going wide with disbelief, then filling with tears, then narrowing with anger. "You...why didn't you save him? What kind of doctor are you?"

"I tried, Kate, I tried. But you've got to understand, we were in the middle of nowhere, and our supplies were low. We'd just come from a village that had a lot of wounded and sick people, and we were on our way to the rendezvous spot for a resupply, when Andrew's truck went over the IED. All of them were hurt, and we had to try to help everyone, all at the same time. We did our best, but Andrew was badly injured. There was nothing I could do for him."

"Did he..." She bit her lip, swiped at the tears on her cheeks. "Did he suffer?"

People asked that question and never wanted the truth. They never wanted to know that their loved one had been in pain, or lingered with a mortal wound. They wanted death to be quick, painless, as simple as closing your eyes. "He wasn't in any pain," Brody said, which was the truth. The one thing they'd had in good supply was painkillers. "And we talked a lot during his last hours."

"Hours? He suffered for *hours?* Why...why didn't you get more help? Call in a helicopter? Do something... else? Why did you...let him die?"

"I didn't let him, Kate. I did everything I could."

"But it wasn't enough, was it?" She shook her head, then glanced down at the card. When she raised her gaze to his, those emerald eyes had gone stone cold. "And so you came here, came to me, on what, a mercy mission? Take care of the grieving older sister?"

"It wasn't like that. I—"

"I don't care anymore, Brody. I don't care what you intended or what you meant. You let my brother die and then you stood in my shop and watched me cry and never said a word." She flung the card at him. It pinged off Brody's chest and tumbled to the carpeting. "Stay away from me. I'm not your pity case anymore."

Then she turned on her heel and headed back into the ballroom. The door shut, and Kate was gone.

CHAPTER TEN

Brody stood beside his brother and watched Riley and Stace pledge till death do us part, with ridiculous, happy smiles all over their faces. Frank, Stace's head chef, longtime friend and business partner, watched from his seat, tears streaming down his face. Gran sat beside Frank, dabbing at her pale blue eyes. Stace's sister and nephew sat on the other side of Frank, beaming like proud parents.

The wedding had been simple, the service lasting just a few minutes, with Brody and Finn serving as ushers. Finn had been best man, and gave Riley a hug of congratulations when he handed the youngest McKenna the rings. As soon as the minister pronounced them man and wife, Jiao, Finn and Ellie's adopted daughter who had served as flower girl, scooted out of her mother's arms, and scattered more rose petals on the altar. The guests laughed, and Jiao ducked back behind her mother again. Ellie chuckled, and wrapped a protective arm around the small dark-haired girl.

The minister introduced Mr. and Mrs. McKenna, then Riley and Stace turned toward the small crowd of guests, hand in hand. Applause and cheers went up, and the couple headed down the makeshift aisle in the center of the diner, while guests showered them with rose petals and Jiao brought up the rear, scattering flowers in their wake.

Throughout the wedding, Brody had forced himself to keep his attention on the front of the room. Not to turn back and see if Kate was one of the guests seated in the diner. But now, as Riley and Stace walked away, his gaze scanned the crowd, searching for long brown hair, deep green eyes.

Disappointment sunk like a stone in his gut. She wasn't here.

He'd hoped, even though he had heard the finality in her voice, but still he'd hoped that she would change her mind. His heart kept looking for her, kept hoping to see her when there was a flash of dark brown hair or the sound of laughter.

The band began playing, and several waitstaff hurried in to move the seating around to accommodate a dance floor in the center of the diner. The cupcakes had been delivered early this morning, probably part of Kate's plan to avoid him. Before Brody arrived, she'd stacked them on a towering stack of circular plates, decorated with fresh flowers and strands of iridescent pearls, like a real wedding cake. As always, Kate had surpassed expectations. The guests oohed and aahed, and Riley pointed to Brody. "Don't tell us, tell my brother over there. I believe he made each one himself."

"It wasn't me," Brody said, "it was all the work of—"

The door opened. Kate strode inside. She had her hair up in a loose bun, with tendrils tickling along her jaw. She wore a pale blue dress that floated above her knees in a swishy bell, and floral heels that accented her legs, curved her calves. Brody reminded himself to breathe.

He couldn't dare to hope for forgiveness for lying to her for so long, regardless of how many times he'd apologized. But a part of him was damned glad to see her, and wishing anyway.

"Thank that beautiful woman there." He pointed at Kate. "Kate Spencer, the owner of Nora's Sweet Shop, which makes amazing cupcakes and chocolates."

Several guests swarmed Kate, singing her praises over the floral decorated cupcakes. She thanked them, the admiration causing her to blush. After a while, she broke away from the group, accepting a glass of champagne from a passing waiter. She chatted with Ellie while Brody watched and wished she was talking to him.

Riley strode over to Brody. "I see your baker is here. You going to ask her to dance?"

"She's not my anything." She never had been, really. The relationship he'd built with her had been built on a lie, and everyone knew a castle constructed on sand would never last.

Riley arched a brow. "What happened?"

"I told her about Afghanistan. That I was the doctor with her brother when he died. And that her brother had asked me to watch out for her."

"How'd that go?"

Brody scowled at his little brother. "How do you think?"

"I'm glad you finally talked about it, Brody."

"Yeah, well, I'm not. Now I've lost her, and all because I was trying to do the right thing."

Riley clapped a hand on Brody's shoulder. "Remember

when you and me tricked Finn into seeing Ellie, with that old bait and switch we did with the bagels?"

"Yeah." Brody watched Kate across the room. Stace had moved on to greet other guests and now Kate stood away from the crowd, sipping her champagne, and watching the guests. Avoiding all eye contact with him.

"You need to do the same thing, and find a way to get that pretty girl to talk to you again."

"She doesn't want to see me."

"Did you ask her?"

"Of course not. I just assumed—"

Riley let out a gust. "Geez, Brody, now I'm the expert in relationships in this family? If that's the case, then you'd better check the sky, because I think pigs are flying. You don't assume, brother, you go find out. You have to get in there and take a shot before you can score."

Brody arched a brow. "Did you just tell me to score?"

"Hey, I may be grown up and responsible and married now," he sent a wave over to Stace, "but I'm not perfect." Riley gave Brody a nudge. "Now go over there and take a chance. The woman really likes you. Lord only knows why, but she does." He grinned. "So don't let her get away, or Finn and I will have to take charge."

Riley joined his wife. Brody waved off the waiter's offer of champagne and threaded his way through the tables and chairs until he reached Kate. Up close, she looked a hundred times more beautiful. With her hair up, he could see the delicate curve of her neck, the tiny diamond earrings in her lobes. He caught the scent of vanilla and cinnamon, and a bone deep ache to hold her rushed through his veins.

Brody headed over to her. "Can we talk?"

"I think we've talked all we need to," Kate said, her tone short, cold. "Our business is concluded, and I've found out who you really are. What else is there to discuss?" She raised her eyes to him. Hurt and disappointment pooled in those emerald depths.

"Kate, let me explain."

"Why? What are you going to tell me that's going to change anything?"

"Just hear me out. Please. Five minutes, that's all I ask."

She bit her lip, considering. "Fine. Five minutes."

A start. Right now, Brody would take any start he could get.

"Let's get out of here, okay?" He led her through the diner, into the kitchen, then out the back door and into the alley that ran behind the Morning Glory. He propped the back door open with a rock, then turned to Kate. The sun danced off her hair, shining on those tempting curls, and it was all he could do not to take her in his arms. "I'm sorry for not telling you who I was right off the bat. I was wrong."

She shook her head, tears welling in her eyes. "You should have told me."

"I know. You're right." If he could have done it differently, he would have. All this time, he'd thought he was doing the right thing, but he hadn't been. Looking at Kate now, at the hurt in her face, he wished he could start over. "That last conversation I had with Andrew, when he knew he was dying, he asked only one thing of me."

She raised her gaze to his. "What?"

"That I make sure you were okay. That you were moving forward with your life. He said he was afraid you'd be stuck in your grief. He begged me not to tell you the truth because he was afraid it would make things worse for you."

"Worse? How can knowing the truth make it worse?"

Brody wanted to reach for Kate, but he held back. "He was afraid you would blame yourself all over again. He said you told him that if anything ever happened to him, you'd feel responsible."

She nodded. "I did say that. And he was right. If I hadn't—"

"The last thing he wanted was for you to think you were the reason he was over there." Brody reached for Kate's hand. "Andrew loved his job, and he loved you. He didn't join the military because of you, he joined because he was doing what he does best."

"What's that?"

"Protecting the people he loves. He was doing it then, and he's been doing it ever since he died, through me." Brody let go of Kate's hand and dropped onto the concrete stoop to face a few self truths. "I can relate, because that's what I've done all my life. I've protected my family. Protected myself. I nag my grandmother about getting checkups, harass my brothers about annual physicals. I take care of those around me, because if I do, I can..."

"Prevent another tragedy."

"Yeah. Or at least that was my plan. I thought I went into medicine to change people's lives," he said, "but in reality, I did it to change my own. When my parents died, I remember thinking how powerless I felt. One minute they were here, the next they were gone. I didn't have any say in it. I didn't have any control over it."

"You were eight, Brody. There was nothing you could do."

"Try telling that to an eight-year-old whose world just turned inside out. I became a doctor, I think partly as a way to change that history. You know, save someone else's loved ones and do it often enough, and it would make up for my loss. But it never did. I kept thinking if I could find the right prescription, make the right diagnosis, it would be enough. Change a life, in some small way. And most of all, control the risks, as best I could."

"And thus control the outcome."

He nodded. "But then I went to Afghanistan and realized that sometimes you have to let people take risks. If your brother hadn't been the one in the lead, if he and his team hadn't hit that bomb, it would have hit us. And those villagers would have died. He gave his life for us, because that was his job. He protected us, by risking himself."

She bit her lip. "That was Andrew. He did it all his life."

"You once called him a true hero, and I agree. He was an example for the rest of us to live up to," Brody said. "When that patient of mine at Mass General died, I had to go and tell the family. It was my first notification and the attending thought it would be a good idea for me to learn how. The whole thing was…agonizing. Horrible. The patient's sister was there, and his mother and father, and all I remember seeing was the grief in their eyes. I knew I was causing it, by my words, and I couldn't stop it, because it was the truth. There was no going back and bringing that man back to life. Or bringing him back to his family."

"But you're a doctor. You deal with life and death

every day. Why was this any different?" She took two steps closer and bent her knees until they were eye level. "I *deserved* to know, Brody. You lied to me, over and over again. Why would you do that? To me? Why couldn't you—"

"Because he was my *friend,* damn it!" The last words ripped from Brody's throat, leaving him hoarse. All those weeks he'd spent overseas with Andrew by his side, he'd imagined the two of them meeting up again in Newton, sitting down to watch the game, have a few beers, trading stories about their time in the Middle East. He'd never expected that a bright, sunny morning in the middle of fall would be the day Andrew Spencer, that vibrant, strong young man, would breathe his last breath. "I watched my friend die and it tore me apart. It was like I was losing a brother. I kicked myself for every decision, every moment. I wanted to go back and undo it, to change the course of destiny, and I couldn't. I couldn't do it, Kate, no matter how much I wanted to." He ran a hand through his hair. "I thought it was hard losing that first patient, but at least there, I had all the tools I needed, all the medical staff I could want. The best hospital, the best tests. When he died, I knew I had done everything I could. But when Andrew died—" Brody cursed and turned away.

"What about when Andrew died?"

Brody was back there again. The heat of the Middle East a powerful, shimmering wall. At every turn, the smell of poverty, desperation, lost hope. "We were in this tiny little dirt floor hut in the middle of nowhere. Hours from a hospital. There was me and one other inexperienced doctor, and that was it. No X-ray machines. No operating rooms. No specialists on call. We'd just come from a village that had a lot of sick and wounded people, and our supplies were low. If I'd been in a hospital, I could have hooked him up to a machine. I could have bought him some time. I could have…" He cursed again. The ground blurred before him.

"Changed the ending?"

Brody closed his eyes and drew in a long, deep breath. All these weeks, the what ifs had plagued him. He'd replayed the entire day a hundred times in his mind, but in the end, always came to the same conclusion. The one ending that in his heart he couldn't accept, even though he knew it was the only one. No matter how many hospitals or experts had been on the scene of that explosion, the outcome would have been the same. Sometimes, people just died. And it sucked, plain and simple. "No. He had deep internal injuries from that bomb. The best hospital in the world would have only been able to do one thing." He lifted his gaze to Kate's. "Buy him more time."

"To do what?" Kate asked. "To suffer?"

"To say goodbye."

And there, Brody realized, lay the crux of what had dogged him all these weeks. What had kept him from sleeping. What had laid guilt on his shoulders like a two-ton wall. "I wanted him to have time to talk to you. The cell service where we were was non-existent, and I kept hoping he'd get well enough that we could transport or that a signal would magically appear. I just wanted Andrew to have time to tell his family he loved them. I didn't want to be his messenger, damn it, I wanted him to talk to his family himself. He tried to hold on, he really did, I could hear the helicopters in the distance and I kept hoping, and praying, and trying to keep him alive." Brody's voice broke, and he raised his gaze to her. "But I couldn't fix this, Kate. I…couldn't. I failed and I'm sorry, Kate. I'm so, so sorry."

She buried her face in her hands. Her shoulders shook with her tears, and Brody got to his feet, wrapped an arm around Kate and drew her to him. She tensed, then finally leaned against him. She cried for a long time, Brody doing nothing more than holding her and running a hand down her back and whispering the same thing over and over again. *I'm sorry.*

He could have said it a thousand times and never felt like it was enough. Finally, her tears eased, and so too did the stiffness in her body, the tension in her features. She drew back, the dark green lakes of her eyes still brimming. "Don't you understand, Brody?" she said. "My brother did say goodbye to me and did tell me he loved me. He did it through you."

Perhaps. But had Brody done all he could have to ensure Andrew's final message had been delivered? "The only thing I could do afterwards was fulfill his last wishes. It wasn't enough, but it was all I had, and for a friend like Andrew, I couldn't let him down again. I wasn't a very good messenger. I should have…" he threw up his hands, "done more."

"Sometimes you do all you can and you accept that it's enough. You said something like that to me just the other day. Remember?"

He could hear the band playing inside, music celebrating a new beginning, a new life, while outside in the alley, he and Kate were discussing a loss and trying like hell to move forward with their own lives.

"I'm a doctor," he said. "I'm supposed to heal people. It's in the Hippocratic Oath, for God's sake. Do no harm. And I did harm by treating him in the middle of nowhere, in a place that didn't have everything I needed. I did him harm by not giving him the time to say good-bye." He cursed and shook his head. "I did my best, and I fell short. Maybe I'm not the doctor I thought I was."

"Let me ask you something." She laid a hand on his. "What would have happened to my brother if you hadn't been there? If he'd been alone and that bomb went off?"

"He'd have suffered. It would have been long and slow, and painful." A horrible, undeserved end for a hero like Andrew.

"And you eased that pain, didn't you?" Kate asked.

"Yes. We had plenty of painkillers."

"I meant you eased that pain by talking to him. By making him forget what was happening. He didn't suffer because he had you. A friend, when he needed one most." She held Brody's hand tight in her own, her touch a soothing balm for his tortured thoughts. "Thank you for being with him. Thank you for taking care of him. Thank you for making it easier for him."

The words came from Kate's heart. She didn't blame him. She'd absolved him. "He cared about you deeply. I wish I could have brought him home to you."

Tears spilled from her eyes. "I do, too."

His entire goal for the last few weeks had been to help her move forward, to help her go after her dreams, and even if she never spoke to him again after today, he wanted to know she was at least driving down that path and he had done what Andrew asked of him. Then he could take satisfaction in that. He told himself it would be enough. "You have to move forward, Kate. Rent that building. Expand the business. The one thing Andrew wanted more than anything was for you to be happy.

For you to go after your dreams. We stood in that shop in Weymouth and I could see in your eyes that you wanted to take that chance, but in the end, you walked away. You've stood still for weeks, Kate, instead of taking the leap."

"I wasn't the risk taker. That was Andrew. And without him—" She shook her head. "I can't do it. Nora's Sweet Shop is doing just fine where it is. I don't need to expand."

"Because you're afraid of failure."

"I'm done." She turned away. "I didn't come here for you to tell me what I'm doing wrong with my life."

"You're just going to run away? Because the conversation got tough?"

"I'm not doing that, Brody." She pressed a finger into his chest. "You are. Quit telling me how to change my life until you have the courage to change your own." She crossed to the door and jerked it open.

She was about to leave, and he knew, as well as he knew his own name, that he would never see her again if he let her go now. He had done what he always did— protect, worry, dispense advice and medicine—and had been too afraid to do the same for himself.

Doctor, heal thyself, she'd joked.

How true that was.

If he didn't change now, he'd lose everything that mattered. Brody was tired of losing what was important to him. Not one more day, not one more minute, would he live afraid of the risks ahead. Afraid of loss. Afraid of being out of control.

"Kate, wait." He let out a gust. She lingered at the door, half here, half gone. "We're two of a kind, aren't we? Both in fields that require us to take a chance every day, and both of us too scared to do that. You would think I wouldn't be, because I've seen risk and loss firsthand, felt it under my hands, heard it in the slowing beep of a heart rate. But I am. I'm scared as hell to lose a patient. And scared as hell to lose you."

"Me? Why?"

"Because you're the first woman I've ever met who has shown me my faults and dared me to face them. You're right about me. About my need to fix everything. I think it's part of why I do the medical missions. It wasn't enough to change lives here. I needed to do it in other towns, other countries. And I thought I was doing just fine." Now the words that he had always kept to himself, the tight leash he had held on his emotions, uncoiled, and the sentences spilled out in a fast waterfall. "Until I went to Afghanistan. There, I was stuck in the middle of nowhere with a dying man and a roomful of wounded. Not enough time, not enough supplies, not enough medicine in the world to save everyone. Medicine couldn't save him, and all I could do was watch him die." Brody ran a hand over his face. "I have been scared, all this time, of not having control over the situation. Of exactly what happened with your brother." He took in Kate's delicate features, her wide green eyes. In the past few weeks, she had changed him in dozens of ways, by encouraging him to step out his normal world. He wanted more of that. More of her. And that meant changing, right this second. "I'm done being afraid of risk, Kate. It's kept me from doing what truly makes me happy."

"Like what?"

"Like expanding the medical missions to be bigger, to take on new challenges. Like doing more to change the lives of the people here in Newton. And most of all," he paused, "like falling in love."

"Falling in love? You have?"

"A long time ago." As he said the words, he realized they were true. "I think I fell in love with you before I even met you."

She shook her head. "That's impossible. How could you do that?"

"Andrew and I talked about you all the time. Whenever we were between towns, or between shifts, we talked. He told me all about the shop and your grandmother, and you." Brody grinned. "He made you sound like Mother Theresa and Santa Claus, all rolled into one."

And finally, Kate laughed and Brody saw a bit of her fire return. "I'm not that nice or that altruistic."

"He thought you were. And the more he talked, the more I saw you through his eyes. I saw you in the care packages you sent. In the notes you wrote. In the memories he shared. And I thought, damn, what would it be like to have someone love me that much?" He took her hands in his and held tight. "It took me over a month to work up the courage to walk into your shop. I would walk down there every day during my lunch break, and after I got done for the day, and every time I would turn around. Partly because I was dreading telling you who I was and why I was there, and partly because I was afraid I'd meet you and you wouldn't be what I imagined."

"I wouldn't live up to the hype?"

He smiled. "Something like that. But then I met you, and you were all Andrew said, and more. You were kind and funny and smart and beautiful. Very beautiful." He closed the gap between them and took both her hands in his. "More than I deserved. More than I ever hoped."

"Brody—"

"You knocked me off my feet so badly that first day, I didn't even realize I picked out a sports basket for my grandmother, who is as far from a sports fan as you can get. All I knew was that I wanted to talk to you, wanted to get to know you. And…" He let out a breath, and faced the last bit of truth. That for all these years, he had held back from love, protecting his own heart, because of one failure. Which had cost him true happiness. No more. "I want more of that, Kate. I want you. In my life now and for always."

She shook her head and broke away from him. "Brody, I can't do this right now. I'm supposed to be at the wedding, and so are you, and—"

He reached for her again, this time cupping her face with his hands. "Take a risk with me, Kate."

Her eyes grew wide, and her cheeks flushed. "I…I can't." She shook her head. "You need to quit believing in the impossible, Brody McKenna, and look at the facts. We're not meant to be together. We started out on a lie, and you can't build anything from that. Nothing except goodbye."

Then she headed back inside. The door slammed shut with a loud bang that echoed in the alley for a long, long time.

CHAPTER ELEVEN

THE ruined cupcakes sat on the counter, mocking Kate. Distracted and out of sorts, she'd burned two batches this morning. She'd thought coming in on a Sunday would allow her to get caught up, but it had only put her further behind. When Joanne had come in to help, Kate almost burst into tears with relief. "I hate to abandon you on your first day back," she said to Joanne, "but I really need to get some air. I think I'll go for a run."

"Go, go. I'll be fine. Besides, your grandmother is due to stop by for her daily sugar fix. She'll keep me company."

Kate tossed her apron to the side and headed out to the front of the store. Just as she did, Nora entered, making a beeline for the cupcake display. She placed a small box on the counter beside her, then lifted the glass dome. "Good morning, granddaughter."

"Good morning." She pressed a kiss to Nora's cheek. "How are you?"

"Just fine, just fine, or I will be when I get my daily cupcake." Nora's hand hovered over the red devil, then the peanut butter banana, then the chocolate cherry. "Off to see the cute doctor?"

"No. I'm just heading out for a run."

"Well, before you go, maybe you should open this package. I found it on the doorstep when I came in." Nora settled on the chocolate cherry, and replaced the glass dome. She leaned against the counter, peeled off the paper wrapping and took a bite. "Amazing. As always."

"That package is for me?" Kate grabbed a box cutter from under the counter. Maybe she'd ordered something for the shop and forgotten. She slipped the knife under the tape, and as she peeled it off, she realized the box had no stamp, no delivery confirmation tag. And it was Sunday, a day no service delivered. "You just found it out front?"

"Yup." Nora took another bite, and smiled. "Delicious. Sometimes the best and sweetest one is the one you missed, in your rush to make a choice. Don't you think?"

Kate peeled up one flap, then the other. She reached into the cardboard container and pulled out a small black velvet box. A card had been attached to the top, and she opened that first.

Sometimes all you need is a little luck before you leap.
—Brody

"What do you have there?" Nora asked.

"I don't know." Kate pried open the hinged lid of the box, and let out a gasp when she saw the contents. A four leaf clover, a real one, encased in a glass dome, and attached to a heart shaped charm, dangling from a wide silver ring. A keychain, waiting for keys.

"That man knows you well," Nora said.

"He does. But—"

Nora laid a hand on Kate's shoulder, cutting off her words. "Before you go spouting off all the reasons why you shouldn't love him, let me ask you something. Did I ever tell you the story of who named the shop?"

Kate nodded. "Yeah, but tell it again. It's my favorite."

A soft smile stole across Nora's face as she talked. "When we were first married, your grandfather knew how much I wanted to open a little shop like this, but I was young and had a child on the way and a husband going off to war, and the whole idea just scared the pants off me. The day he left, I woke up and found a spatula on my pillow. Tied up with a bow. He'd carved Nora's Sweet Shop into the handle. Did it by hand, with a pocketknife I gave him for his birthday. He told me the sweetest thing I could ever do for him was to go after my dreams. And I did. I never regretted it, not for a second. I've been so proud to see you and Andrew take up the reins and carry that dream forward." Nora put a hand on Kate's. "Now it's your turn to run with the ball and carry it the rest of the way. To take Nora's to new heights."

"I'm scared, Grandma." Kate ran her hands over the silver ring. "What if I fail?"

"Just by having the courage to go after your dreams, you've already won, my dear." She drew her granddaughter into a long, tight hug. "And no matter what, I'll be here to support you."

Kate fingered the charm, then lifted her gaze to the newspaper article on the wall. Andrew seemed to be smiling his support from across the room. He would want her to do this. To move forward, and as Brody had said, quit standing still. "Thanks, Grandma."

"You're welcome. Now go for that run, and clear your head. I'll stay here and," she lifted the glass dome and snagged a peanut butter banana cupcake this time, "guard the cupcakes."

Kate laughed. She slipped the keychain into her pocket then headed out the door. A few minutes later, she had stopped at her townhouse, changed her clothes, and started toward the reservoir. The Sunday morning sunshine warmed her, and she found herself slipping into the rhythm and peace of running.

Her mind drifted to Brody and she found herself looking for him, hoping to see him running, too. The keychain bounced in her pocket, a reminder of his gift. A little luck to encourage her to take a risk.

A risk like opening a second location?

A risk like…

Opening her heart?

She rounded the bend of the reservoir, startling a flock of pigeons. They burst into flight, with a chatter of wings. The contingent of pigeons circled away, opting for greener pastures, while several settled back onto the ground in Kate's wake. She watched the ones in flight, their squat bodies becoming sleek gray missiles against the sunny fall sky.

Her steps slowed. She glanced to her right, and saw two paths. One that led toward home. One that led another direction. The opposite from the one she'd always taken. Kate drew in a breath and started running again.

The smell of braised beef filled the kitchen of Mary McKenna's Newton house. Finn, Ellie and Jiao stood in the sunroom and talked with Mary, while Brody hung back in the library and pretended to look for a book he had no intention of reading.

His attempt to show Kate he cared, that he supported her, had gone bust. He'd dropped off the package early this morning, tempted to deliver it in person, but not sure what kind of reception he'd get. After the way things had ended yesterday, he wasn't sure she ever wanted to see him again. Still, he couldn't get her out of his mind, no matter how hard he tried.

"Come join us, Brody," Ellie said to her brother-in-law. "Your grandmother's about to open a bottle of that '92 Merlot you like." She rubbed a hand over her stomach. "Though I'm sticking to apple juice for a while."

Brody waved off the offer. "I'm not in a wine mood tonight. I'll be out shortly."

Ellie sighed and leaned against the doorjamb. "You McKenna men are all the same." A soft smile stole across her face. "Stubborn, determined and impossible."

"Hey. How's that supposed to make me feel better?"

"It's not." Ellie pushed off from the door and crossed to Finn. Her pregnancy had just started to show, giving her a tiny bit of a curve to her belly. "Those are the qualities I love the most in Finn. He's like a bulldog, only cuter."

Brody laughed. "I don't know about the cute part."

"I heard what you did." Ellie paused before him. She took the book in his hands away and shoved it back on the bookshelf. "Both in Afghanistan and with Kate. I think you did the right thing."

He shook his head. "I lost her in the end. How is that the right thing?"

"You were doing what all three of you do. Protecting

her. Taking care of her. She'll realize that and come around."

"I hope so."

"She will." Ellie laid a hand on Brody's arm, the loving support of a sister-in-law who had already become an indelible part of the McKenna family tree. "And it'll all work out. A wise man once told me that the smart man lets the woman he loves go, so that when she returns, it'll be because she truly loves him." She poked a finger at his chest. "That smart man was you. That day in the coffee shop, remember?"

"I do." He and Riley had dragged Finn down there and surprised him with Ellie, all in hopes of spurring the two to work it out. Which, clearly, they had. "Thank you, Ellie."

"You're welcome."

"You're a smart woman," Brody said.

She laughed. "Well, be sure to tell Finn that."

"I think he already knows."

Ellie smiled, the same private smile that Brody had seen on Riley, Stace and Finn. The smile of someone deeply in love and happy as hell.

She gave his arm a gentle tug. "Come on, Brody, have a glass of wine with your family and have a little faith that it will all be okay."

He headed out of the library and into the hall with Ellie. "You do know I'm a doctor, right? Faith is a hard commodity to come by in a world of tests and logic."

"I know. But you're also an Irishman and if anyone trusts in luck and faith, it should be you." She gave him a grin, then stepped away and waved toward the front door.

Brody turned. Kate stood in the doorway, wearing a

T-shirt, shorts and running shoes. A fine sheen of sweat glistened on her skin. To Brody, she'd never looked more beautiful or desirable. He caught his breath.

"I'm sorry for just showing up, but…" she bit her lip and gave him a tentative version of a smile, "does that offer for a family dinner still stand?"

Joy burst in his heart and he closed the distance between them in a few short strides. "Yes, every Sunday. Two on the dot," he said, then let out a gust. "Oh, God, Kate, I wasn't sure I'd see you again."

"I got the package." She reached in her pocket and held up the keychain. It tick-tocked back and forth on her finger. "Thank you."

"You're welcome."

She turned it over in her palm, and dropped her gaze to the small green leaves. "When I got it, my first instinct was to do what I've always done. To run from the risk and the fear. And I literally did just that."

"I can tell." He grinned. "But you still look sexy, even after a run."

"I thought running would help me forget," she said, "but all I did was look for you. At every turn, at every stop. I didn't want to run around the reservoir. I wanted to run to you, Brody. And so…"

"You did." If happiness were a meter, Brody's would shoot off the charts. "I'm glad."

"You were right. I was scared. When I was a kid, I was the one who had to be the steady rudder for Andrew. And he worried about me. The two of us, taking care of each other. Our parents fought all the time and it was just…chaos. I didn't want my little brother to worry or get scared, so I became the practical, dependable one. I let him dream big, and I kept my feet firmly on the ground. Then when he died, it shook me badly. So I did what I do best, and kept those feet cemented in place. I thought if I did everything the same, no surprises, no risks, I wouldn't have to experience that kind of loss or pain again. But I was wrong. Because in the end, it cost me you."

"I'm still here, Kate." He brushed a tendril of hair off her forehead. "And I always will be."

"When you told me you'd fallen in love with me, all I could see was this big cliff and you standing beside it, asking me to jump with you. I got scared and I ran, instead of doing what I should have done."

"Which was…?"

She smiled and winnowed the gap between them, lifted her arms to wrap around his neck and raised on her tiptoes. She pressed a kiss to his lips, then drew back. "That."

"Much better than walking away." He tightened his hold on her, then kissed her back. God, he loved this woman. Loved her smile. Loved her smarts. Loved everything about her. "Much, much better."

"I got scared, because I fell in love with you, too. I found a hundred reasons not to be with you, because I couldn't believe that a man like you really existed. One who could light fireworks inside me and at the same time understand my deepest needs." She tangled her fingers in his hair and her eyes shimmered with emotion. "A real hero."

He glanced away. "That's not me."

"It is." She drew his face around until he faced her again. "You saved my brother. And you saved me. You put everyone else ahead of you and you took the risks no one else wanted to take. That's a hero to me."

He still disagreed about the real hero here, but if the woman he loved saw him as one, he wouldn't argue. To Brody, Kate was the heroic one, determined and smart, the one who had saved him from an empty life. He cupped her jaw, and ran a thumb along her chin. "I love you, Kate Spencer."

A smile burst across her face, bright as the sun. "I love you, too, Brody. I think I fell for you the minute you brought that silly basket up to the counter for your grandmother."

He chuckled. "I was too distracted by you to make a smart buying decision."

"Good thing." She grinned. She held up the key ring again. "You know, there's only one thing this ring needs now."

"What?"

"Keys to a second location. As soon as I get home, I'm calling that realtor. There will be a Nora's in every town, or at least a lot of them." She laughed.

"And I'm thinking of taking on a partner for the practice, so I can keep treating people here in Newton, but also step up my mission work."

She smiled. "Both of us, taking risks."

"Together. The best way to do it."

She laid her head against his chest. "I agree, Brody. I agree."

"The best choice I ever made was that basket. And… you." His heart, no his entire world, were complete now with Kate in his arms. He could see their future ahead, one where she brought smiles to people everywhere there was a Nora's Sweet Shop, and he healed the sick and wounded in far-flung places. There would be some compromises ahead, making both her business and his mission trips work, but Brody had no doubt they'd find a way because in the end, he and Kate had the same core values. The same goals. To create a world full of heroes. And he couldn't wait another minute to start on that path. "I meant what I said. I want to spend the rest of my life with you. Will you marry me, Kate?"

She drew in a deep breath, then exhaled it with a smile. "Yes, I will, Brody."

A burst of applause sounded from behind them. Brody turned to find Finn and Ellie, flanked by his grandmother and Jiao, all clapping and beaming their approval. "I only have one thing to say," Finn said, crossing to his middle brother. "It's about damned time."

Brody laughed. "Always direct and to the point, Finn."

Finn drew Kate into a hug, so tight she squeaked. "Welcome to the family, Kate. The McKennas are a rowdy bunch, so be prepared."

"For what?" Kate asked.

"For the happiest time of your life." He clapped Brody on the shoulder, offered the two of them congratulations, then headed for the dining room. "Now let's eat."

* * * * *

COMING NEXT MONTH from Harlequin® Romance
AVAILABLE OCTOBER 2, 2012

#4339 THE ENGLISH LORD'S SECRET SON
Margaret Way

Seven years ago Ashe left Cate heartbroken. Now he's back...but is he prepared for a secret that will change *everything?*

#4340 THE RANCHER'S UNEXPECTED FAMILY
The Larkville Legacy
Myrna Mackenzie

Taciturn cowboy Holt turns his *no* into *yes* when Kathryn demands that he save the local clinic—and, annoyingly, also attracts his attention!

#4341 SNOWBOUND IN THE EARL'S CASTLE
Holiday Miracles
Fiona Harper

Faith has never found a man more infuriating *and* attractive than aristocrat Marcus! Trapped in his castle, she finds him suddenly hard to resist....

#4342 BELLA'S IMPOSSIBLE BOSS
Michelle Douglas

Babysitting your boss's daughter doesn't mean you have to like her! Dominic's risking his reputation, but does Bella know it, too?

#4343 WEDDING DATE WITH MR. WRONG
Nicola Marsh

There's something about her ex, Archer, that has always tempted Callie to throw caution to the wind... but hasn't she learned her lesson?

#4344 A GIRL LESS ORDINARY
Leah Ashton

Billionaire Jake knows the real woman beneath Ella's glamorous transformation, and sparks fly as the past evokes unforgettable memories!

You can find more information on upcoming Harlequin® titles, free excerpts and more at www.Harlequin.com.

HRCNM0912

REQUEST YOUR FREE BOOKS!
2 FREE NOVELS PLUS 2 FREE GIFTS!

Harlequin
Romance

From the Heart, For the Heart

YES! Please send me 2 FREE Harlequin® Romance novels and my 2 FREE gifts (gifts are worth about $10). After receiving them, if I don't wish to receive any more books, I can return the shipping statement marked "cancel". If I don't cancel, I will receive 6 brand-new novels every month and be billed just $4.09 per book in the U.S. or $4.49 per book in Canada. That's a savings of at least 14% off the cover price! It's quite a bargain! Shipping and handling is just 50¢ per book in the U.S. and 75¢ per book in Canada.* I understand that accepting the 2 free books and gifts places me under no obligation to buy anything. I can always return a shipment and cancel at any time. Even if I never buy another book, the two free books and gifts are mine to keep forever.

116/316 HDN FESE

Name	(PLEASE PRINT)	

Address		Apt. #

City	State/Prov.	Zip/Postal Code

Signature (if under 18, a parent or guardian must sign)

Mail to the **Reader Service**:
IN U.S.A.: P.O. Box 1867, Buffalo, NY 14240-1867
IN CANADA: P.O. Box 609, Fort Erie, Ontario L2A 5X3

Not valid for current subscribers to Harlequin Romance books.

**Are you a subscriber to Harlequin Romance books
and want to receive the larger-print edition?
Call 1-800-873-8635 or visit www.ReaderService.com.**

* Terms and prices subject to change without notice. Prices do not include applicable taxes. Sales tax applicable in N.Y. Canadian residents will be charged applicable taxes. Offer not valid in Quebec. This offer is limited to one order per household. All orders subject to credit approval. Credit or debit balances in a customer's account(s) may be offset by any other outstanding balance owed by or to the customer. Please allow 4 to 6 weeks for delivery. Offer available while quantities last.

Your Privacy—The Reader Service is committed to protecting your privacy. Our Privacy Policy is available online at www.ReaderService.com or upon request from the Reader Service.

We make a portion of our mailing list available to reputable third parties that offer products we believe may interest you. If you prefer that we not exchange your name with third parties, or if you wish to clarify or modify your communication preferences, please visit us at www.ReaderService.com/consumerschoice or write to us at Reader Service Preference Service, P.O. Box 9062, Buffalo, NY 14269. Include your complete name and address.

HRI1B

HARLEQUIN® Romance

At their grandmother's request, three estranged
sisters return home for Christmas to the small town
of Beckett's Run. Little do they know that this family
reunion will reveal long-buried secrets…
and new-found love.

Discover the magic of Christmas in a brand-new
Harlequin® Romance miniseries.

In October 2012, find yourself
SNOWBOUND IN THE EARL'S CASTLE
by **Fiona Harper**

Be enchanted in November 2012 by a
SLEIGH RIDE WITH THE RANCHER
by **Donna Alward**

And be mesmerized in December 2012 by
MISTLETOE KISSES WITH THE BILLIONAIRE
by **Shirley Jump**

Available wherever books are sold.

*Sensational author Kate Hewitt brings you
a sneak-peek excerpt from THE DARKEST OF SECRETS,
the intensely powerful first story
in her new Harlequin® Presents® miniseries,*
THE POWER OF REDEMPTION.

* * *

"You're attracted to me, Grace."

"It doesn't matter."

"Do you still not trust me?" he asked quietly. "Is that it? Are you afraid—of me?"

"I'm not afraid of you," she said, and meant it. She might not trust him, but she didn't fear him. She simply didn't want to let him have the kind of power opening your body or heart to someone would give. And then of course there were so many reasons not to get involved.

"What, then?" She just shook her head. "I know you've been hurt," he said quietly and she let out a sad little laugh. He was painting his own picture of her, she knew then, a happy little painting like one a child might make. Too bad he had the wrong paint box.

"And how do you know that?" she asked.

"It's evident in everything you do and say—"

"No, it isn't." She *had* been hurt, but not the way he thought. She'd never been an innocent victim, as much as she wished things could be that simple. And she knew, to her own shame and weakness, that she wouldn't say anything. She didn't want him to look at her differently. With judgment rather than compassion, scorn instead of sympathy.

"Why can't you get involved, then, Grace?" Khalis asked. "It was just a kiss, after all." He'd moved to block the doorway, even though Grace hadn't yet attempted to leave. His face looked harsh now, all hard angles and narrowed eyes, even though his body remained relaxed. A man of contradictions—or was it simply deception? Which was the real man, Grace wondered, the smiling man who'd rubbed her feet so gently, or the angry son who refused to grieve for the family he'd just lost? Or was he both, showing one face to the world and hiding another, just as she was?

Khalis Tannous has ruthlessly eradicated every hint of corruption and scandal from his life. But the shadows haunting the eyes of his most recent—most beautiful— employee aren't enough to dampen his desire. Grace can foresee the cost of giving in to temptation, but will she risk everything she has for a night in his bed?

Find out on September 18, 2012, wherever books are sold!

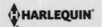